Praise for the Samantha Kidd Mysteries:

"...the book is enriched by the author's cleverly phrased prose and convincing characterization. The surprise ending will satisfy and delight many mystery fans. A diverting mystery that offers laughs and chills." *-Kirkus Reviews*

"an impressive cozy mystery from a promising author." - *Mystery Tribune*

"A really funny mystery with a chicklit feel." -Susan M. Boyer, USA Today Bestselling Author of *Lowcountry Bordello*

"Designer Dirty Laundry shows that even the toughest crime is no match for a sleuth in fishnet stockings who knows her way around the designer department. A delightful debut." -Kris Neri, Lefty Award-Nominated author of *Revenge For Old Times' Sake*

"Combining fashion and fatalities, Diane Vallere pens a winning debut mystery...a sleek and stylish read." -Ellen Byerrum, National Bestselling author of the Crime of Fashion mysteries

"Vallere once again brings her knowledgeable fashion skills to the forefront, along with comedy, mystery, and a saucy romance. *Buyer, Beware* did not disappoint!" -*Chick Lit Plus*

"Fashion is always at the forefront, but never at the cost of excellent writing, humorous dialogue, or a compelling story." -*Kings River Life*

"A captivating new mystery voice, Vallere has stitched together haute couture and murder in a stylish mystery. Dirty Laundry has never been so engrossing!" -Krista Davis, *New York Times* Bestselling Author of The Domestic Diva Mysteries

"Samantha Kidd is an engaging amateur sleuth." -*Mysterious Reviews*

"It keeps you at the edge of your seat. I love the description of clothes in this book...if you love fashion, pick this up!" -*Los Angeles Mamma Blog*

"Diane Vallere takes the reader through this cozy mystery with her signature wit and humor." -Mary Marks, *NY Journal of Books*

"...be careful; you might just laugh right out loud as you read." -3 no 7 Looks at Books

TOUGH LUXE

A SAMANTHA KIDD MYSTERY

Copyright Page

TOUGH LUXE

Book 11 in the Samantha Kidd Mystery Series

A Polyester Press Mystery

Copyright © 2021, Diane Vallere

e-ISBN: 9781939197894

Paperback: ISBN: 9781939197900

Hardcover: ISBN: 9781954579170

TOUGH LUXE

A SAMANTHA KIDD MYSTERY

DIANE VALLERE

Polyester Press

To Philadelphia Pretzel Factory, Snyder's of Hanover, Tom Sturgis, and Unique Splits pretzels. I love you all!

CHAPTER 1

Money Opens Doors

MONEY, AS THEY SAY, OPENS A LOT OF DOORS. IN THIS case, the door that opened for me belonged to the Berks County Correctional Facility for Females. It cost me little more than my reputation as a local amateur sleuth who attended the same high school as Suzy Kintz, the prisoner who extended the invitation.

Considering Suzy was an heir to the Kintz pretzel fortune, her money probably opened a lot of doors too. Just not the very heavy one that had kept her inside for close to two decades. And to be accurate, it was her lawyer who extended the invitation, not Suzy, but he made it clear it was her idea.

One week ago, a letter from the law offices of Brewster & Case was delivered to me at the *Ribbon Eagle*, the newspaper where I wrote an occasional column on style. The opportunity for the column came about on the suggestion of a reporter who'd written a profile on me after my involvement in a string of homicide investigations became impossible to ignore. I accepted for the sheer fun of it; an unexpected windfall had changed my tax bracket and left me, for the first time in my life, with the luxury of not stressing about money.

The prison invitation was accompanied by instructions on the date and time of our proposed meeting. I'd thought it was a practical joke. I waited twenty-four hours before calling Suzy's attorney to confirm and did so from the privacy of my current loaner car while going through an automatic car wash. If it were a joke, then the jokester wasn't going to get their payoff while I was in public.

Turned out, the invitation was legitimate.

The Berks County Correctional Facility for Females, or BCCFF as nobody called it ever because those letters don't make up a pronounceable word, sat on a stretch of land north on Route 222, otherwise known (to me) as the road to the good ice cream shop. Somewhere past the strip malls of Ribbon, interspersed with farms and corn fields, sat a compound that housed women who'd been convicted of major crimes. Like Suzy, most of them were in there for life.

I sat in the passenger-side seat of my husband (and favorite shoe designer) Nick Taylor's white truck. Nick sat behind the wheel. The stress of working nonstop on his start-up sneaker collection, Saint Nick, tired him, and the tolerance with which he treated my unusual activities had been wearing thin. (Marriage is awesome, by the way, but having a roommate makes it harder to participate in covert and questionable activities.)

Last night, while he was under the influence of fettuc-cini alfredo and my new lace-trimmed nightie, Nick offered to give me a ride to the prison. Me being under the influence of his root-beer-barrel-brown eyes and the romantic full moon, accepted.

This morning, Nick wore a dark-amber French terry sweatshirt over a white tee, soft, worn-in jeans, and white leather sneakers. Last week's stubble had officially turned a corner into beard territory. The crinkles around his eyes had grown deeper, and not because he'd spent the past six months grinning over his success.

It was one thing for Nick to help me out me when my life was in freefall; he'd saved me from danger more than once. (I'd saved him from danger too, but pride goeth before the fall, so I stopped reminding him about it after our first month of marriage.) But his shoe business had crashed and burned, around the same time my car suffered a similar fate, and the sneaker venture was turning out to be more work than he'd originally thought. His offer to drive me today had been sweet at the time, but under the cold light of day, he seemed less enthused about the time my activities were taking out of his day.

"Tell me again why we're here," Nick said. "Is this for the paper? You never mentioned that you applied to visit a prisoner."

"A lawyer contacted me through the newspaper office. He sent a letter saying someone I knew in high school put me on her approved visitor list. I filled out the application and approved the background check and here we are."

"Do you know where you're supposed to go?"

"The letter said to arrive between eight and eight thirty and park in the visitor spaces outside the prison. There were no instructions about when to enter, but I found visiting hours on the prison website." I glanced at the dash-board clock. "We're early."

"Because you're excited," Nick said. He allowed a smile. "You're a funny woman."

"It's a prison," I said. "For women. Some of the women inside killed people." A thought I hadn't yet considered crossed my mind. "You don't think any of them are serving time because of me, do you?" My reputation as an amateur sleuth did not come without having interacted with the local criminal element.

"I think if you recognize anybody, you should pretend you don't. Don't think of this as a Meet-Up group."

The building in front of me was the sort of gray-beige concrete that conjured up images of asylums, which, in this case, was both chilling and accurate. It was a flat-roofed job built around the time shirtwaist dresses and pearls were the everyday norm. A round overhang supported by white columns framed out the entrance. Under any other circum-stances, it might have been described as majestic. Under these, it just looked cold.

To the left of the main building was an attached two-story, boxlike structure. Small, square windows were evenly spaced along the roofline but nowhere below. I stared at those windows for close to a minute before concluding the building was probably where the prisoners slept.

In contrast to the unimaginative color of the building was a lush green yard that stretched from the perimeter of the prison to the parking lot. I hadn't seen grass that green since watching the Masters golf championship with Nick's dad. There was something about the color palette — beige and green — that would have made a nice backdrop for a fashion photo shoot.

"What's her name?" Nick asked idly.

"Suzy. Suzy Kintz."

He tightened his grip on the steering wheel. "Of Kintz pretzels? The one who murdered her husband?"

I nodded.

Suzy Kintz, would-be heiress to the Kintz pretzel fortune, was serving time for the murder of her husband, Trenton Vega. Though she maintained her innocence, enough evidence had stacked up against her that the prosecutor secured a guilty verdict without breaking a sweat. That was seventeen ago.

Whatever chances there might have been for Suzy to get a retrial were dashed when a second body, eight miles from the initial crime scene, was discovered the same night. The prosecution argued the murders were related, and the jury had agreed. A term of twenty-five years to life had been tacked on to her initial sentence, meaning even with good behavior, her chances at seeing an early release were nonexistent.

Countless reporters had tried, and failed, to arrange interviews with her over the years. When I asked her lawyer why I'd been contacted, he said his job was to make the arrangements. Any further explanation would come directly from her.

Nick switched off the radio. "You never mentioned you were friends with Suzy Kintz," he said.

"Didn't I?"

"I'm pretty sure I'd remember if you did."

"We weren't friends," I said absentmindedly. "We

weren't enemies either. We just traveled in different circles."

Or more accurately, I traveled in my circle, and Suzy traveled by herself.

I'd grown up in Ribbon, in the very house that I'd bought from my parents a few years ago when I chose to give up my life in New York and simplify (ha!). I'd hung with a crowd that cared more about music and clothes than deep learning. It wasn't until after I went to college that I discovered I could turn a lifetime of reading *Vogue* into a future; a major in the history of fashion combined with a minor in business led me to a lucrative career as a shoe buyer for a top luxury store.

Suzy had joined our class in the tenth grade after being expelled from a Pennsylvania prep school. I still remember the day she first arrived in a shiny white convertible Audi Cabriolet that was a rumored sweet sixteen gift. Instead of eating lunch in the cafeteria, she drove off by herself and returned for sixth period.

From the moment she became my classmate, she was the girl everybody liked but nobody knew. She had an innate sense of style that didn't follow magazine or shopping mall conventions, but always looked great. I remember eagerly waiting to see what she wore to school. She seemed unaware of my fan-girl attention. She was physically there but not present all the way through graduation. I wondered, briefly, what almost two decades of incarceration had done to her sense of style.

I was so lost in my thoughts about high school and Suzy's fashion sense that I didn't see the man who appeared alongside of Nick's truck. His closed fist pounded on the window and I jumped and spilled coffee on the leg of my skirt. Nick pulled a stash of napkins out of his door. I grabbed them and dabbed at the stain.

The man stared into the window, first at me and then Nick and back to me, and either the caffeine overload, the adrenaline rush, or the general excitement over entering a correctional facility made my hand shake while I lowered the window.

When I finally succeeded, the man spoke. "You need to move your car over there," he said. He waved his hand toward a far corner of the parking lot that was rapidly filling with cars.

"I thought these were the visitor spaces," I said.

"Not enough spaces today." He looked annoyed. Instead of answering my question, he leaned forward and looked past me to Nick. "Move your truck to the press lot. Get your equipment and take a seat in one of the folding chairs."

"I'm here to visit with a prisoner," I said. I reached into my handbag and pulled out a folder that contained the letter from Suzy's lawyer.

The man shook his head. "The prison's in lockdown. No visits. There's one thing happening at this prison today, and that's the press conference. If you have a letter telling you to be here, then that's where you want to be."

Lockdown? Press conference? It appeared as though my invitation wasn't the stuff of class reunions.

CHAPTER 2
Press Conference

"Move your car or leave. Doesn't matter to me. Just don't park it here." The man straightened and walked away.

I closed my window and watched his receding back. Nick put the truck into reverse and backed up, then drove toward the lot the man had indicated. A line of cars, from beat-up sedans to energy-efficient hybrids, inched forward to fill the vacant spaces. At this rate, I'd be late for my scheduled meeting time.

"Let me out here," I said. "It's closer to the entrance, and you won't have to deal with trying to find a space."

"How long do you think you'll be?" Nick asked.

"I don't know. Whatever I thought this was, it looks like it wasn't. If you need to leave, I can call a cab."

Nick looked at the dashboard clock. I could feel his conflict radiating off him. "I'll wait here," he said. He held up the latest issue of *Footwear News*. "Plenty to keep me busy."

We kissed goodbye, a modest peck, and I climbed out. The driver of a dingy silver Toyota Camry let Nick cut through and turn toward the exit, then pulled forward and parked on the end of a row of cars. A man in jeans and a striped dress shirt under an unconstructed dark-gray blazer got out of the Camry. He held an equipment bag, which he slung over his shoulder.

"You here for the press conference?" he called out to me.

"I don't know. I thought I was here to visit a prisoner."

"Which one?"

I hesitated for a moment. "Suzy Kintz," I said in a low voice.

"Yeah, you're one of us. We're both screwed on camera placement. My two-year-old spilled coffee on my first shirt and I had to change. What's your excuse?" He glanced at my outfit. "You always dress like that to cover a story?"

I didn't want to admit to a perfect stranger that I'd followed the advice of a popular blog about prison life that gave tips on a visitor's dress code. The most challenging to follow was the avoidance of gang colors, which sent me off on an internet search to find out what those were and then an online shopping spree to procure an ensemble that avoided them all.

I was left with one safe choice. Apparently, pink wasn't big in the gang community.

"I got dressed in the dark," I said, adjusting the peplum on my knit top so it lay flat against the waistband of my matching pencil skirt. The man's long stride quickly overtook mine and I fell behind. I hoisted my handbag onto my shoulder and picked up my pace. "I don't understand," I said when I caught up to him. "Who are all of these people? Why are they here?"

"You're a reporter, right?"

Hardly. "Sure," I said.

"So is everybody else. Did you receive a letter from the law offices of Brewster & Case?"

"Yes, but—" I stopped talking abruptly and looked out at the mass of people who'd congregated in the prison yard. All around me, people were setting up tripods, speaking into cameras, taking pictures of the prison, and holding up light gauges while pivoting in circles. A news van pulled into the parking lot, and when the side door slid open, two men climbed out. The driver met them by the back, where they unloaded what appeared to be a portable mission control. I watched as they trudged through the grass to the back of the seating area. A blonde in a sleeveless yellow dress trailed them. Despite the soft breeze that gently swayed the flags by the entrance, nary a hair on her head moved out of place.

"Who are you with?" the man asked.

"I'm by myself."

He laughed. "That's not what I meant. I'm Joey, by the way. Joey Carducci. With the *Philadelphia Post.*"

"You came here from Philadelphia?" I asked. "Philly isn't in Berks County."

"No, but Suzy Kintz is bigger than Berks County." He laughed. "To some people in Philly, Kintz pretzels are a staple. Like Goldenberg Peanut Chews." He jerked his chin toward the crowd of reporters while he adjusted his collapsible tripod. "Some of these people are from Baltimore, some from Jersey. That guy over there is from New York."

"I'm Samantha Kidd," I said, half paying attention to Joey. "*Ribbon Eagle*."

"That's local. Man, you're lucky. This story is in your back yard. I'd love to go through your archives for background. I'm surprised you didn't finagle a way inside before we got here."

I turned from the crowd and assessed Joey directly. "I don't get it. What's the big deal with today? Tell me again why you're here?"

Joey's friendly nature shifted, and he suddenly seemed wary of me. With one question, I'd gone from being an equal to being a liability. His eyes swept my outfit again, and this time his opinion seemed less amused and more turned off. He picked up his tripod and looked over his shoulder. "I think the light is better on the other side of the chairs."

I'd committed a reporter faux pas, and I had no idea what. But with the crowd rapidly filling in, the vacant chairs were fewer and fewer, and even if Joey chose to abandon his new friend (me) and carry his equipment to the other side of the field, he'd be in a much worse position than the one we had staked out by accident. I put my hand on his tripod and held on tight so he couldn't move.

"I'm a columnist. I went to high school with Suzy Kintz, and when the invitation to come here today came to the paper, I thought it was strange but curious. I don't know why she wanted to talk to me, but that's what I thought. That she wanted to talk to me."

"You really don't know, do you?" he asked. Again, his demeanor shifted, this time to amazement.

At that moment, a man in a cheap blue suit took the stage. The breeze caught his silver hair and swirled it around his forehead. He switched on a microphone and cleared his throat and then addressed the press pool. "Good morning. Wow, we pulled a big crowd today." He looked over his shoulder at a woman in a similarly colored pantsuit. She stood erect, with her hands behind her back. Her build was stocky, and her hair was dark gray streaked with white. It was her lipstick, a sharp shade of dark red, that stood out from the rest of her appearance.

"Thank you all for coming," the man said. He held his hands palm-side out toward the crowd. "If you could all take your seats, we can get started." With his left hand, he smoothed his hair away from his forehead, but as soon as he removed his hand, the breeze caught the shiny strands and tossed them around again.

A man in a uniform came out of the prison and glanced at the woman with red lipstick. He showed her something written on a piece of paper, and she shook her head. It was a slight gesture, but I was certain I'd seen it. The man shifted his attention to the speaker. The man in uniform thrust the paper in front of the man who appeared to be in charge, who was left with no choice but to stop talking mid-sentence and look at the proffered note. He read the contents without taking the paper in hand, looked up at the man in uniform, and shook his head like the woman had done. Whatever instructions were on that paper, the two people who had taken the stage seemed to disagree with them.

The crowd, who'd been instructed to take their seats, grew antsy while the new drama played out onstage. A few stood back up and took pictures of the prison and the trio on stage. Considering I had no idea I was expected to attend a press conference, I felt no compulsion to do anything more than observe everyone else.

Finally, the people on stage seemed to reach an agreement over their course of action. The man in charge snatched the paper from the uniformed man's hand and turned back toward the microphone.

"Sorry about the interruption. We're going to get started in a moment. But first, is there a Samantha Kidd in the crowd? Samantha Kidd, from the *Ribbon Eagle*?"

I felt the heat drain from my face. Whatever mistake had brought me to the prison this morning had just been discovered, and I was on the verge of a public shaming.

Joey elbowed me. "That's you, right?"

I nodded.

"Say something."

Reluctantly, I raised my hand. "I'm Samantha Kidd," I said, too low for the man on stage to hear.

"Samantha Kidd is over here," Joey said in a voice about five times louder than the one I'd used.

The crowd's attention shifted to me, and the heat that had left my face flooded back, making me warm under my pink skirtsuit. The man on the stage shielded his eyes and then gestured for me to come forward. "Come on up here, Ms. Kidd. You've been preapproved for an interview."

I glared at Joey, and he winked. "Dinner's on me if you say I'm your photographer," he said. He stood and grabbed his tripod.

"I think I'll keep this scoop for myself," I said with a smile. I left Joey and the other reporters and met up with the man in uniform, who led me inside the prison.

CHAPTER 3
Special Treatment

I'D BEEN IN THE THIRD ROW OF THE AUDIENCE, SO IT was a short walk to the stage. The man in the uniform descended the stairs to the side of the stage and met me on the sidewalk. "Samantha Kidd?" he confirmed.

"Yes," I said.

"Peter Genovese. I'm the head of the Treatment Department. You're here to visit Suzy Kintz, correct?"

"Yes," I said again, this time with some relief. "I tried to tell them at the gate — "

"It's going to be a busy morning. The parking team was told to instruct everyone to go to the back lot. The press knows that, but there's always somebody who tries to get away with claiming to be a visitor so they can get a scoop."

Despite being singled out from the crowd, I felt guilty. It was exactly what I'd done: parking in the visitor space, trying to plead my case to the parking attendant, and arguing with Joey that I should get special treatment. He'd laughed, but it turned out I was right. I was getting special treatment. While the entire press pool of the tristate area was seated outside, about to receive newsworthy information, I was being led inside for a one-on-one conversation.

When yearbooks had been passed around, I boldly asked Suzy to sign mine. If this were a trial to determine our friendship, her inscription would do little more than confuse a jury. She'd simply written: "Play it again, Sam," a *Casablanca* reference that isn't in *Casablanca*. Asking her what she'd meant implied she meant something, but it was just as possible that she thought the notion of writing platitudes to an acquaintance wasn't worth the effort of original thought.

But while I was gearing up for SATs and filling out college applications, Suzy was getting ready to broaden her world view. She showed no interest in the pretzel monopoly that put the Kintz family name on the map and put her trust fund to good use, leaving town the day after graduation.

After college, I left too. Thanks to a job at Bentley's New York, my world also got bigger. I lived in New York, traveled to the various fashion capitals, and rose up the corporate ladder.

And now, twenty plus years after the last time I saw her, Suzy Kintz and I, two girls from Ribbon High, were about to talk inside a correctional facility.

Peter led me to a desk where I handed over my completed application and showed my ID, then we went to a row of lockers. He opened one. "Lockers rent for a quarter. You'll need to put your personal belongings in here. You can take a notepad and pen if you want, but no recording devices, including cell phones, are permitted. No weapons, drugs, or alcohol."

I opened my bag and pulled out a three-inch-by-three-inch notepad with a picture of Barbie on the cover, and a pink ballpoint pen that, embarrassingly, matched my outfit. With as much confidence as I could muster while holding objects a sales department had designed and marketed toward fourteen-year-old girls, I closed my bag and put it in the empty locker. Peter, impressively, didn't show signs of judgment. He closed the locker, turned the key, and handed it to me.

The interior of the Berks County Correctional Facility for Females matched the exterior: beige, gray, and mauve. There were no inspirational quotes posted on the walls and no uplifting colors. I didn't want to think about what it did to a person's mental state to be surrounded by such blandness every day of their lives; I also didn't want to think about what the inmates had done to be there. Once, while embroiled in a hiring snafu that turned into a murder investigation with me as the main suspect (What? It happens...), I'd feared that this might become my reality. Every day, when I wrote in my journal, I declared gratitude for my freedom. My life coach said I should continue the process indefinitely to ensure I avoided backward momentum.

Despite the initial communication of the rules of visitation, Peter was taciturn. Nerves sometimes make me chatty, and I wouldn't have minded him acting like a tour guide. But after answering my first two questions with simple yes and no answers ("Do the inmates get many visitors?" and "I don't suppose you have a coffee cart?"), I stopped asking. We walked down a bright hallway. The leather soles and heels of my shoes made *clack clack* sounds against the vinyl tile floor. Peter glanced at my feet but kept his thoughts to himself.

We walked past several closed doors. I tried to peek inside, but Peter kept up a brisk pace, and not only did my shoes make noises, they made it difficult to keep up.

"Have you ever been in prison before, Ms. Kidd?" Peter asked.

"No. Why? What have you heard?" He glanced at me quizzically. "No," I repeated, and this time I let the one word stand.

"Here's what's going to happen when we enter the visitation quarters. A guard will pat you down, make sure you're not carrying any illegal objects or substances. When they're finished, you'll be fingerprinted, sign in, and be given credentials. From there, you'll take a seat. The prisoner will be searched both before and after your visit, so if you try to pass her something, she, or you, or both of you, will be caught. Do you understand?"

I gulped. My throat was dry, and the effort left a lump in place. I needed a glass of water, but the idea of asking for anything was less than appealing. I held my closed fist to my mouth and coughed, and then forced another swallow.

"Yes," I said.

"Good. In here." He held a door open, and I entered a room.

There are experiences in life that we like to talk about, that we want to savor and we can't wait to share with our friends. Times when we're in the moment but also aware that what's happening is something we might never get to repeat. I've had a lot of those moments, and a fair share of them had led to this one. But being patted down by a prison guard while I stood with my feet spread and my hands against a wall wouldn't make the top one hundred.

I'd edit this part out when I told Nick about my day, I decided right then and there. Unless he wanted to reenact the process.... My nervous thoughts turned blue, and I flushed, and then immediately remembered where I was and tensed.

"Relax. This is a pat-down, not a strip search," the guard said. She cocked her head and assessed me then nodded twice. "Sign in and take a seat. The prisoner will be in shortly."

I did as instructed and sat. I doodled a shoe on my Barbie notepad and then studied my surroundings. The room was clean but dingy like the rest of the building. Walls of exposed concrete had been painted over with high-gloss white paint. Tables and chairs sat intermittently throughout the room, far enough apart to allow conversations, but close enough to remove the concept of privacy. I hadn't known what to expect, but a lifetime of movies had painted a picture of chairs on opposite sides of a thick pane of glass with phones on which we would speak. This room, with a commissary cart along one wall and a bookshelf of videos and magazines, was like the waiting room at a doctor's office.

I sat alone for what was probably ten minutes, though the lack of clocks made it feel like hours. The longer I sat, the more I wanted to get up and wander around, grab a magazine, and settle in, but that wasn't why I was there.

The truth was, I didn't know why I was there. I didn't know what was happening outside. I felt as out of place as if I'd been brought here against my will, and no amount of positive inner-talk was going to change that. If ten minutes in the visiting room of a correctional facility got into my

head, then I couldn't begin to imagine what a life sentence
— or two, as Suzy's case was — would do to me.

A buzzer sounded, and I felt, rather than heard, the
doors to the room unlock. Peter Genovese entered first,
blocking the person behind him. I sat up straighter. This
was it. He stepped aside, and Suzy Kintz, former classmate
and convicted killer, strode toward my table.

CHAPTER 4
In Control

"Samantha Kidd," she said. Her voice was soft. "Thank you for coming."

Suzy was dressed in khakis. The collar of her shirt was flipped up, and the bottom three buttons of the shirt were undone. Her trousers were khaki too, oversized and worn low on her hips. The hems had been torn out and frayed. Her shoes were white sneakers that would have been appropriate in a yoga studio.

"Thank you for having me," I said automatically. "I mean, thank you for — I mean, you're welcome?"

She pulled a chair back and sat down opposite me. "Is that a question?"

"I don't know. I'm not sure what to make of all of this."

"You and me both," she said. Her eyes shifted from my face to my top. "You checked the dress code."

"I did."

I'd spent a fair amount of time wondering what prison had done to Suzy, and I was more startled to discover how familiar she still seemed. She had long brown hair that hung to her waist. Somehow, the ends appeared thick and healthy, not damaged or split. The color was dark brown. Her face was fuller than I remembered in high school, but not so much as to hide her cheekbones or angular jaw. She had what beauty magazines refer to as a square face. Her lips were pink, and when she rested her face, her mouth opened and her two front teeth protruded slightly, like Claudia Schiffer's. Her skin was pale, almost translucent, and her brows were thin and arched in an expert style that seemed impossible to recreate in the real world, let alone in here.

"You want something?" she asked. She pointed over her shoulder at the commissary. "Coffee, tea, water, soda?" She was confident. At ease. I half expected her to gesture to the commissary employee and place an order as if we were in a restaurant.

"No thanks," I said.

Despite declining, she left me at the table and returned with two bottles of water and a pack of cigarettes. She opened the pack and lit up, not asking if I minded the smoke.

"You know what seventeen years in prison does to you?" she asked, as if reading my mind. She answered her question before I could answer. "It forces you to think differently. Out there, people sleepwalk. They go through the motions, and when they go to bed, they don't even remember how they spent their day." She took a long drag on her cigarette, held the smoke in her lungs for a moment, and then exhaled in a long stream of smoke over my head. She pulled the ashtray closer and stabbed out the cigarette then moved the tray to the table behind us.

"You didn't have to put it out for me," I said.

"What makes you think I did?" she asked. "If I cared if it bothered you, I would have asked."

I bristled. This whole visit had been her idea. I'd come along out of curiosity, but I hadn't expected animosity. "Is this how you entertain yourself? You invite people from high school to come visit and you demean us?"

She studied me for a few seconds without speaking. As uncomfortable as I was, I stared back and kept my mouth shut. I was here and I wanted to know why, and if this was why, then this visit was going to set a record for brevity.

"You've never visited anyone in prison before, have you?"

"Is that so hard to believe?"

She stood up and carried the full-minus-one-cigarette pack to the trash. She tossed them and emptied her barely smoked cigarette from the ashtray too. She moved with the same grace and ease that she'd had in high school. Whatever prison had done to her, it hadn't changed that.

When she sat back down, she smiled. "I take one drag on a cigarette every day. When the smoke enters my body, I'm aware of my lungs, of every breath I take. It puts me in the moment. And when I put it out, it reminds me that I'm in control over what happens to me, not anyone else."

"You didn't ask if the cigarette would bother me because you knew you were going to put it out."

She nodded slowly, as if she were the wise teacher and I were her pupil.

It was an odd observation, but as soon as the thought entered my brain, I flashed back to tenth grade, in the locker room before school started. I'd snuck a colorful eyeshadow palette from my sister's vanity and arrived at school early to apply the makeup before homeroom, but the colors I chose left me looking garish. Suzy, the new girl, came in and saw me at the row of mirrors. She took the palette from me and set it down, then pulled a makeup wipe out of her handbag and used it to remove the colors I'd painted on my face. It had been an awkwardly intimate moment for a tenth grade girl.

When the colors were gone, she picked up the palette. "Close your eyes," she said. I complied. I felt the brush against my left eyelid, soft and gentle, and then on my right. "Open and look up," she said. I realized that I trusted her completely, though I didn't know a thing about her. "Mascara?" I handed her a tube, and she swiped that onto my lashes. She capped the tube and handed it back. "You're done."

I looked in the mirror and immediately saw myself differently than I ever had before. She'd shied away from the bright colors that I'd first applied and used plum shades that contrasted with my green eyes. I looked like me, but better. Enhanced.

"Thank you," I said.

She'd smiled, not a huge grin, but a knowing smile that said, "I know something you don't, and you want to know what it is." It was the same smile she gave me now. Funny, that very same attitude was what the press grabbed onto when she was found guilty of murder.

I lost track of Suzy after high school until I spotted her name on editorial content in *Luxe*, a low-budget magazine dedicated to fashion, beauty, and decorating. I'd been in college at the time, and reading fashion magazines was a hobby, not a job requirement.

The article in question was about the impact of grunge on the fashion world. At the time, Kate Moss was the reigning queen of the runway circuit, heroin-chic was the rage, and any savvy person could match the trend pages with a quickie shopping trip to Woolrich. Plaid flannel and ribbed undershirts became the new poet blouse, and the shampoo industry reported record lows as unwashed hair became a thing. Lines between high fashion and no fashion blurred, and the trickle-up impact of streetstyle created a reverse economic dilemma. Those with money were at a loss. Who was this Doctor Martin and why did everyone want his boots?

Suzy took on the fashion industry in a cheeky manner by commissioning a wardrobe made of shirts from Goodwill. She turned the idea of grunge into couture, but it was *her* couture, mismatched plaids pieced together into pantsuits, pencil skirts, and, in the case of her garment for the museum gala, a ball gown. She paired it with a boy's secondhand blazer from a local prep school. When more than one designer copied her look for their runway shows the following season, she surprised everyone again by donating the pieces to a charity fundraiser and adopting a wardrobe of a white Gap T-shirt under a men's suit paired with suede Gucci loafers. Aside from the red carpet, this became the only outfit she was ever photographed in again — until circumstances dressed her in prison sweats instead.

"No," she said. "I don't get my kicks by inviting people from high school to the prison. I don't invite people to prison."

"You invited me," I said.

"True," she said.

Something kept me from coming out and asking why. I couldn't put my finger on it, but I felt like I was on a job interview.

"What do you know about me?" she asked abruptly.

"Your family owns a sixth-generation pretzel company—"

"Not my family. Me. My story. My circumstances. What do you know about it?"

"Not a lot," I admitted. "I lived in New York when you were, you know."

"Arrested. You don't have to be shy about it. Every person in this prison already knows I was arrested for murder, including me. Do you know any of the details?"

"No. I didn't keep in touch with people from high school."

"But you're back," she said. "How come?"

"I had a great job, but I wasn't happy. My parents wanted to move to the west coast, and I bought their house, gave up my career, and moved back to Ribbon."

"That's crazy," she said. "You know that, right? Most people move back to their hometowns to be closer to family. You waited until yours left."

"It's not like I was avoiding them."

"You sure about that?"

"Why am I here?" I asked instead of answering her question.

"You tell me."

"No, you tell me. You arranged this. You don't talk to the press. You don't trade on your family name for publicity.

You don't grant interviews. But you wanted to talk to me, and I want to know why." This time, when she stared at me, I stared back. I could play chicken too.

Suzy picked up her bottle of water and toyed with the cap. "Last night, a lifer from Rikers Island admitted to killing a hiker in Ribbon, Pennsylvania seventeen years ago."

"Seventeen years ago," I repeated. Aside from that fact, she could have been talking about an episode of *Forensic Files*, but those words gave her information context. "The second victim."

"So you *do* know something about my case," she said.

I nodded.

She continued. "I was found guilty of murdering my husband. I'm serving a second life sentence without the possibility of release because of that second body. Now that there's irrefutable evidence to prove the murder of that hiker was unconnected to me, I want the courts to reevaluate my case. I used to think I was going to die in here. I made peace with it a long time ago."

"But now?"

"Now there's a chance for me to get out, and I want your help."

CHAPTER 5

Visions of Do-Gooder Justice

"I'M A FORMER FASHION BUYER," I SAID.

"Don't sell yourself short, Samantha," Suzy said. "You've got a reputation around these parts."

"These parts?"

Suzy indicated her surroundings. I admit, the idea of being a local celebrity to a women's prison was a little thrilling. Visions of do-gooder justice and fighting against the man flitted through my imagination like a Taylor Swift video.

"Prison's given me more spare time than I'm used to. I saw your name in the paper, and it reminded me of high school. I asked the prison librarian to pull some research on you, and I found out you've done more than write a column about fashion. The experience you picked up since moving back is fitting to my current situation."

"I suppose it is." I glanced around the room where we sat. "Are you the only person getting a visit today?"

She pointed behind her. "That press conference is about me. It's going to create some attention, and attention elicits less-than-desirable reactions. The treatment manager made arrangements for the other prisoners to have their visits in the library."

"Peter Genovese?" I asked. "I met him this morning."

She shook her head. "You don't 'meet' people in here. You interact with them. He's in charge of how the prisoners are treated, and that means he gets to do whatever he wants as long as word doesn't get out." She shrugged, as if this were one of many lessons she'd learned and accepted.

I leaned forward and dropped my voice. "Is he corrupt?"

"Corruption is hard to prove. He does his thing, and the governor leaves him alone."

"Has he, um, tried anything with you?"

"I'm not his type." Suzy was calm, jovial, even, discussing the prison staff like he was the homeroom teacher. There were multiple ways to interpret Peter Genovese's type, but that seemed the least important aspect of my visit. Suzy asked me here to talk about her case, but so far, that was the one subject we'd barely broached.

"Tell me about that night," I prompted.

She leaned back in her chair and focused on her water bottle for a few seconds and then sat up and pushed it away. "Trenton and I made plans to come here for Thanksgiving. My parents have a farm on the northwest side of Ribbon. When Trenton and I visited, we stayed in the guest cottage."

"He seemed more like the five-star-hotel type."

She shrugged. "It's quaint by New York City standards, but I grew up here, so it's familiar." She uncapped her water and took a swig. "My sister had reservations for us for dinner."

"I didn't know you had a sister," I said. "Did she go to Ribbon High too?"

"No. Unlike me, Dawn didn't get kicked out of prep school." She delivered a wry smile and appeared to indulge in a memory, and then the gentle visage that the mention of her sister had brought on disappeared. "I finished up at the magazine early, but Trenton got stuck with a client. He told me to leave without him and he'd get here around midnight."

"You drove to Ribbon separately?"

Suzy shrugged. "We were both on edge." She was quiet for a moment and then looked at me directly. "We had a fight. It wasn't unusual; we fought a lot. Sometimes it led to good sex. Sometimes it didn't. When he said he had to meet with a client and couldn't leave, I left without him. It's a two-and-a-half-hour drive on a good day, and the mood I was in, I didn't mind the traffic."

"You said you had dinner plans. The night before Thanksgiving?"

"Thanksgiving is a meal like any other meal. It's not a mandate for gluttony. Don't you eat every day?"

"My eating habits probably shouldn't be cited when establishing a standard," I said, recalling the two donuts I'd had in the car.

She grinned. "I remember that from high school. You always had an appetite. Nice to know some things haven't changed."

(It was two and a half donuts. I split the third one with Nick.)

"Our dinner plans turned into something bigger," Suzy continued. "My sister invited an old friend at the last minute. I was in a crappy mood and wasn't up for a reunion."

"You could have canceled."

"And be at the cottage for round two when Trenton arrived? No, thank you." She got quiet. I couldn't tell if she reviewed that night every day or if this walk down memory lane was one she kept at bay.

After an awkward silence, I prompted her to continue. "You were at dinner..."

"I took a Valium in the parking lot outside the restaurant. I was the last one to arrive, and the table had started drinking without me. I caught up quickly, and the second half of the dinner is a foggy memory."

"How long did the meal last?"

"We were there for a few hours. I offered to pick up the check, but Trenton had called ahead and made arrangements with the restaurant to pay for dinner. It was typical Trenton. Make a good impression even if you don't make the party."

"Did everybody leave together?"

"No. I was exhausted and wanted to go home, but the others stayed. Thanks to the interaction of the Valium and the alcohol, I was in no condition to drive. I left my car with the valet and called a service to take me home."

"What about your sister? Wouldn't she give you a ride?"

"She wasn't ready to leave."

"Was Trenton waiting for you at the guest cottage?"

"No. The cottage was dark. Trenton never said when he was going to leave New York, and between spending the night in a car driving to Ribbon to stay on a farm or blowing off steam with a client, well, I wouldn't have been surprised if he rolled up at four in the morning. I didn't want to wake up smelling like smoke, so I took a shower. When I came out of the bathroom, I found Trenton dead in the bedroom and the gun on the bed. I called 911 and waited downstairs for the police to arrive."

"Where were your parents?"

"Asleep in their house. They both suffer from partial hearing loss from spending their life in a pretzel factory, and they have blackout curtains in the bedroom so they can keep the hours required to run the business."

"They had no idea what happened? Crime scenes are like three-ring circuses. They didn't see or hear anything?"

"I don't know if you've ever seen where my family lives, but it's a seventy-five-hundred-square-foot house on twenty acres of farmland. The guest cottage is half a mile away. The police came to us via a side road that doesn't go past the main house. My parents found out the next day when they were contacted by the media."

The buzzer over the door sounded, and the large prison guard who had patted me down entered. "Five minutes," she said.

Suzy shook her head in the first show of frustration at her circumstances that she'd displayed. She leaned forward. "My husband wasn't a nice man, but I didn't kill him. The evidence looks like I did. That press conference out there is about me. By the time the evening news runs, the whole country will be reminded of the pretzel heiress serving two life sentences. If I get a new trial, the jury pool will be tainted."

"What do you want from me?"

"Do your research. Decide what you want to do. If you come back, I'll answer any questions you ask."

That story would be worth a lot to a reporter. It would make a career. But I wasn't looking to get paid, not from the misfortune of someone I'd once admired. Everything I saw in Suzy Kintz told me she was telling the truth, and I wanted to believe her.

The possibility also existed that she was manipulating me. I'd been involved in some crazy situations since moving back to Ribbon, and several of them had been written up in the paper. My dirty laundry was well known.

If what Suzy said was true, then she'd known for years that I was back in town and occasionally mixed up in crime-solving. Our shared high school experience made me the perfect person for her to tap for help. I was an idealist who remembered her from the days before her personal drama. I liked to help people, and here was a person asking for my help.

Or so it seemed. I was on the fence, unsure which way to proceed. I wasn't a private investigator. I was just a woman who'd had some success asking questions and banging on doors. And lacking the common sense to know when not to insert herself into situations other more practical people would know to avoid. Oh, heck, if Suzy Kintz had read those articles, then she knew everything about me she needed to know.

"Don't give me an answer now," she said. "Contact my lawyer if you want to come back." She glanced at my Barbie notebook and pink pen, and then at my outfit. "Next time you might want to blend."

CHAPTER 6
Like High School

I HAD TOO MUCH WEIGHING ON MY MIND TO GIVE THE exit trip through the prison the same attention I had the entrance. After retrieving my personal belongings from the locker, I went outside and called Nick.

"I'm done."

"How'd it go?"

"I'll tell you in the car." I turned my head and looked over my shoulder at the beige concrete building. The chairs that had been set up for the reporters were being packed up. The platform stage had been dismantled. I'd have to wait until the afternoon news to find out what the press pool had been told, though I doubted their information was as interesting as mine. "Are you still in the lot? Can you pull around?"

"Change of plans. I had to take a call from China. My dad's there. He'll give you a ride. I'll let him know to come to the exit."

Thanks to his involvement with the sneaker industry, trips to Asia had occupied much of Nick's time. In recent months, a travel ban had kept him in the states, and he'd had to find ways to communicate with his team without being present. Technology had served them well, though there was no technological fix for the time difference.

A few years ago, after a hip injury, Nick's dad followed in my footsteps and moved from New York to Ribbon. The two Taylor men were roomies until Nick and I got married. My house became our home, and Nick Senior inherited the apartment and turned it into a senior citizen bachelor pad.

I stood on the sidewalk feeling more conspicuous than I had all day. A few women in khaki button-down shirts and work pants were outside working on the lawn. They were prisoners too, I realized. They were on work detail. I hadn't asked Suzy if she had a job. I hadn't asked her if she had friends inside. I hadn't asked her anything about her day-to-day life, and she hadn't offered. I knew very little more than I knew when I went inside, yet the experience of walking through those doors had shifted my whole perspective.

A few minutes later, a sexy black Maserati pulled up to the curb. Nick Senior sat behind the wheel, nestled on amber leather seats. Bardot, the black French bulldog Nick had given him for Christmas, sat on the passenger-side seat. I opened the door and climbed in, shifting Bardot to my lap. She sniffed me — it seemed I'd picked up some prison smells — and then turned away from me and stared at the women working in the gardens while making snorting noises.

Much like my current carless dilemma, Nick Senior used to rely on Nick when he needed to get somewhere. It made sense when they shared an apartment after Senior relocated from New York, but when Nick moved in with me, his dad lost the ability to borrow the truck. It turns out a seventy-year-old widower can be far more decisive than an almost-forty former fashion buyer when it comes to car choices. The Maserati was preowned and cost the same amount as the Toyota Avalon that was on loan to me at the time, and the day Senior surprised us with the purchase was the same day Nick told me to take my time with my decision and not get distracted by visions of how I might look behind the wheel of an expensive Italian sportscar.

Sometimes I wonder what he really thinks of me.

"They let you out," Nick Senior said. "Junior and I were worried. Was it what you expected?"

"It was like high school." I followed the dog's stare toward the building and considered what must go on behind those walls.

"Your friend has been in prison for seventeen years."

"Not her. The prison. The walls and the floor. The building. It felt so normal."

"What did you expect? *Caged Heat?*"

"You know what I mean. I didn't expect it to feel familiar."

I told Nick's dad about the visit, sharing the information that would be common knowledge when the press ran with the news, but holding onto Suzy's claim of innocence. Her quiet insistence resonated with me, but I wanted to know more before I decided what I was going to do.

"Where are we headed? Your place?" Senior asked.

"Take me to Tanner's Cars on Pottsville Pike."

"Are you ready to make a decision?"

"I'm still considering my options. I'm trying to be practical."

He shook his head at the thought.

Nick Senior turned on the radio and we drove in silence. Even Bardot seemed to feel the change in the atmosphere when we left the prison grounds and headed west. I stroked her short bristly fur and stared out at the passing cornfields and thought about Suzy. She had a chance to get out of prison – the first real chance she'd had since the night she was arrested – and she wanted my help. It would be a difficult favor to refuse.

CHAPTER 7
The Rich Live by Different Rules

Nick Senior pulled into the parking lot of a Toyota dealer and dropped me off outside the showroom. I went inside, and Senior pulled out of the lot. It wasn't a show of confidence in my vehicle decision-making ability, but an understanding of my routine. I hadn't bought a car since, well, ever. The Honda del Sol that had been destroyed had originally belonged to my mom. She sold it to me for cheap when I got the job at Bentley's, and it had spent the better part of my time in New York occupying a parking space in a lot in Manhattan. The mileage was low, the car was cute, and I'd expected to have it a long time. I even kept up with the oil changes.

Enter the local mafia. My car became a casualty, as did my job. I relied on the kindness of friends and taxi drivers (I didn't trust Uber, not with my track record of encountering less-than-savory characters), until a massive windfall changed my net worth overnight. My new financial manager advised me to put the money in a trust that paid me interest quarterly. Aside from a mini Rolex with a pink face and a couple of charitable donations, I left the money in the bank, but my loved ones were starting to drop comments about my vehicular dependency.

"Samantha, come on in." Ian Tanner, the owner of Tanner Auto, held the door to the showroom open for me. Ian was in his late sixties. He wore a plaid shirt open at the collar under a sport coat, khaki trousers, and cognac lace-up oxfords that made no sound on the polished concrete showroom floor. "What are you thinking today? Sports car? I'd love to see you behind the wheel of a Mustang."

"I was thinking something smaller."

"How about a BMW Z4? Two-fifty-five horsepower, goes from zero to sixty in five point two seconds. BMW's most advanced operating system. Plus, it comes in red." He wiggled his eyebrows. "I could see you in a red car."

"Don't red cars get stopped by the police more than any other color?"

"That's an urban legend."

"I don't think I'm a red car person."

He glanced at my outfit. "Not many cars come in pink."

The decision to buy a car turned out to be one I wasn't prepared to make lightly. Ian Tanner recognized this. With the implied understanding that I would eventually purchase something from him, he let me borrow cars overnight to test them out. He called it an advertising move, my daily routine giving his inventory more exposure than it had parked on the lot. I wondered what he'd think about me taking one to the correctional facility on my next visit. Doubtful that would elevate his brand.

"I don't know," I said, chewing my lip. "What else have you got?" I asked.

"How about an electric car? I just got a Nissan Leaf in on a trade."

"Don't electric cars die unexpectedly?"

"That hardly ever happens."

I shrugged. "Okay, I'll give it a shot."

Ian smiled. "I'll draw up the paperwork."

I wandered the showroom while I waited. It was a moderate day of business. Sales associates greeted customers as they walked into the showroom. Ian's son, Kent Tanner, filled out paperwork in his office. The other sales associates knew better than to waste their time trying to sell me on horsepower or chassis specs. Two men smiled and went back to their conversation. I circled a shiny blue floor model of a GR Supra A91 Edition in "Refraction," a shade of blue that was just to the left of cobalt. (I'm not a car person, but the dealer sticker on the rear window makes it easy to sound like I know what I'm talking about.)

A man I'd overheard talking to the service department sat in the waiting area. A salesman I didn't know poured himself a cup of coffee from the self-serve station and then stood near the customer, both watching the news. I went largely unacknowledged despite my pink outfit.

A female reporter mentioned a press conference earlier today. "— new evidence. An inmate at Rikers Prison confessed to killing a hiker in Blue Marsh Lake Park, eight miles from where Trenton Vega was found murdered. Vega's wife, the daughter of a prominent pretzel family, has been serving a double life sentence for both murders. With this new information, it's expected that her lawyer will appeal her sentence and petition for a new trial."

"I heard she posed for Playboy," the salesman said.

"I heard it was a porno," countered the customer.

"I'd like to see that." The salesman glanced over his shoulder and saw me and had the courtesy to look embarrassed.

"She's guilty," the customer said. "I bet she killed them both and made a deal with that guy in Rikers to take the fall."

"He's a lifer," the salesman said. "What kind of a deal would be worth it to him?"

"Do you have any idea how much money the Kintz family has?" asked the customer. "Somebody probably paid him off. Dig into his financials and you'll find a payout to set his family up for life."

I sensed someone had joined me and turned to find Kent Tanner standing a few feet away, watching the monitor. His attention was focused on the news report.

The customer in the waiting area kept up his small talk. "The rich live by different rules than the rest of us." He turned around and saw Kent hovering nearby. "No offense," he said.

"None taken," Kent replied.

A serviceman in blue coveralls walked across the sales floor and told the waiting customer that his car was ready. Together, they walked past us and through a door marked "Service." The salesman stayed behind and topped off his coffee.

I'd spent so much of my time back in Ribbon fighting to pay my bills that it never occurred to me that there were wealthy people living right here, people who made their money from local businesses that had been established generations ago. I had arrived at Tanner Auto because I needed a car and they were the biggest lot in town. It never occurred to me that, like the Kintz family, the Tanners were in the top one percent.

A young couple walked into the showroom, and Kent greeted them. From a few feet away, I overheard the man say they were just looking.

"Do you believe what he said?" I asked the salesman with the coffee. "About the rules being different for the rich?"

"Sure," he said. "Look at you. You think any other customers get to borrow dealer cars indefinitely? Tanner knows you have money. He wants your business. He also wants you to tell your friends to come here and get cars for themselves and their kids."

"I'm not rich," I protested.

He scanned me from head to toe. "You got dropped off by a guy driving a Maserati. You're not exactly brown bagging it, either." He turned and walked away.

———

ABOUT TWENTY MINUTES LATER, I drove a silver Nissan Leaf to the soft pretzel store. I waited in the lobby while a fresh, hot batch came out of the oven, bought five, and left. I didn't have a firm agenda, but I did have questions. There was one person I knew would have answers. And if he didn't have answers, he'd know where to find them. I'd call him a mentor if he agreed to dress a little better (I have a rep to protect), which might be the very reason he refused.

I drove through a series of residential areas and eventually parked in the Kenhorst Plaza parking lot and carried the bag of hot pretzels (minus the one I ate in the car) to a nondescript office that was sandwiched between a Chinese food takeout and a dentist's office. A bell sounded when I entered. The front desk was empty, so I sat down behind the desk and buzzed the main office.

"Loncar," said Detective Loncar.

"Samantha Kidd is here to see you," I said.

He cursed. I tore the paper bag open and turned it around. Loncar came out of his office and glared at me.

"Pretzel?" I offered. "They're still hot. Don't burn your mouth."

I'd met Detective Loncar the same day I found my boss dead in an elevator at work. It was my first day on the job, and it felt like a lifetime ago. Since then, I'd been shot at, beaten up, knocked out, injected with a paralytic drug, and fired. Detective Loncar had been there through most of it, and I'd come to like the man. He'd gotten shot at too, right before his retirement from the police force, and instead of going quietly into the night, he hung out a shingle as a private dick.

"Do those pretzels come with strings?"

"Don't be silly. Sometimes a pretzel is just a pretzel."

He separated a pretzel from the rest (they came out of the oven stuck together) and tore off a loop. I waited until his mouth was full before speaking. "I brought you a case."

He turned toward the trash can and spit out the mouthful of pretzel.

"Hey! Don't waste hot pretzels."

Detective Loncar was a sixty-year-old divorced man who was having a hard time acclimating to single life. He was more TV dinner than dinner out, and his taste in footwear ran toward orthopedic. Today Loncar was dressed in a long-sleeved plaid cotton shirt over a white T-shirt and khaki pants. His belt was brown; his shoes were black. His scowl was the one accessory that he never seemed to change.

He put his hands in his pockets and stared down at me. "You said there were no strings attached."

"I told you, the pretzels are a gift. I was feeling generous. The case is unrelated." I considered Suzy's pretzel family wealth and what the men at the car dealership had said. "There might be a pretzel angle. I don't know yet. I suppose it's safe to say the pretzels are case-adjacent."

"Not interested."

"It's worth your while," I said. I pulled the twist off one of the pretzels and popped the soft dough into my mouth.

"Not interested."

"This could be the thing that shifts your case load from cheating husbands to actual investigation," I said.

"Not interested," he said for the third time.

I leaned back in the office manager's chair and folded my hands behind my head. "Fine. I'll investigate it myself." I waited for him to change his mind. He didn't. I dropped my arms to the desk blotter and leaned forward on my forearms. "How would I go about investigating a murder case that's already been tried?"

"You mean when you can't trip over your feet, stumble onto evidence, put yourself into dangerous situations and almost get yourself killed?"

I think I liked Detective Loncar better when he had to maintain professional banter with the public.

"Sure, if that's how you want to interpret my question."

"If the case was already tried, then it's closed. What's the point?"

"Call it an indulgence in my ongoing education on criminal investigation."

Loncar shook his head. "You need a job."

"I have a job. I work for the paper, remember?"

"Start there. Pull their archives. Find out the facts."

"What if the facts were wrong?"

"If the case is closed, then the police got their man."

CHAPTER 8
Just Like Kinsey Millhone

"Are you ever going to shake this belief that the police are always right?" I asked. "Because in my experience —"

"I'd be careful how you finish that sentence, Ms. Kidd."

Yes, considering Loncar had investigated most of the cases I'd gotten mixed up in, pointing out his sometimes erroneous track record might not be the way to his heart.

I wanted to tell Loncar where I'd spent my morning. I wanted to tell him I'd met with Suzy Kintz. I wanted him to know about the press conference that indicated she might be getting a new trial, that I had an inside scoop into what might become the trial of the century, and that this was bigger than our past collaborations (my word). But I didn't know enough about the case to tell him anything concrete, and for the first time in recent history, it seemed prudent to brush up on the facts before mouthing off.

I stood. "The archives. That's a good idea," I said. I slung my handbag onto my shoulder and stepped away from the desk. "Thanks for the advice. Enjoy the pretzels." I left

Loncar staring after me as I walked to the Nissan and drove away.

It had been a long morning that resulted in a late lunch. Pretzels, while practically a daily vitamin in my book, did not a satisfying meal make. Maintaining my new sense of investigation, I drove though McDonalds for a quarter pounder with cheese just like Kinsey Millhone and ate while driving to the *Ribbon Eagle* headquarters on Penn Street. I parked in the underground lot, finished my fries, balled up my trash, and tossed it in the bin outside the elevators. The scent of fast food clung to my outfit, masking any lingering odors I'd picked up at the correctional facility hours earlier.

When the elevator doors opened, I walked down a short hallway to the main desk. Wendy Shankweiler, a curvy redhead with milky-white skin and several prominent moles, sat behind the desk. "Hi, Sam," she said. She stood and held her arms out. "Business casual with a lunch date. How'd I do?" She slowly turned in a circle so I could see her brown knit dress and boots from all angles.

"Where was the lunch date?"

"The new Greek place."

"Did you have a good time?"

"I had a *great* time."

"Did your date have a great time?"

"We're going out again on Friday."

"Then I'd say you nailed it."

She giggled. "Are you working on Friday? I was thinking of changing at the office."

"Let me check my schedule."

Being the style columnist for the paper came with

encounters just like this. Most of the staff assumed I judged them by their attire. (They were wrong.) (I judged them on their shoes.) (Joke!) (Mostly.) My column was intended to inspire people, not insult them, and I doubted our subscribers read my five hundred words with any regularity. That's what made it fun.

An interesting thing happens when you stop caring what other people think. Suddenly, when not seeking approval, you act like yourself. Your motivations are genuine. Your beliefs bubble up and take form and relate to your life, not that of celebrities with profiles in fashion magazines.

When I first moved back to Ribbon, I'd been concerned about all the wrong things: impressing my boss, holding onto a job, paying my bills. Actually, those were the right things to be concerned with, but along with them came a need to find my place in this world. I'd spent more time than any one person should questioning everything and wondering what it would take to make me happy.

Turns out, happiness is a byproduct of not giving a hoot about what anybody thinks and just doing your thing. After lamenting the lack of readers for my column, that's what I did. I turned it into a challenge where I attended a local event, observed what people were wearing, factored in the activities at said event, and made recommendations for how to bring style to the mix. I'd covered the Chili Pepper Festival, the farmer's market, a local concert series, and most recently a hot-air balloon ride. And thanks to today, I could talk about what to wear to visit someone in jail.

But before I wrote up my column, I had another task.

"Wendy, where would I go to read back issues of the paper?"

"Use the search field on the website. It goes back about five years."

"What if I wanted something older than that?"

"More than five years ago?" she asked, as if anything older than that was not worth knowing.

"Yes."

"Ask Carl." Carl Collins was the reporter who'd gotten me the gig working at the paper. He was a walking encyclopedia when it came to old news, and he was territorial when it came to getting a scoop. Wendy leaned forward and lowered her voice. "Just be careful. If he finds out you're looking for something newsworthy, he'll want the story for himself."

"History of culottes," I said dismissively. "Nothing earth-shattering."

"Okay, but proceed with caution. He was on the warpath today. Something about not getting notified about a press conference at the local women's prison."

Before I had a chance to react, a male voice barked my name. "Kidd. In the conference room. Now."

I turned around and faced Carl. Under any other circumstances, he would have been at the prison this morning instead of me. I hadn't known about the press conference when I arrived at the correctional facility and judging from the drawn eyebrows and tight mouth on Carl's face, he hadn't known either. And it appeared as though he wasn't willing to chalk it up to a humorous set of circumstances.

CHAPTER 9

Too Stupid to Live

"Hi, Carl," I said. "I guess you heard about Suzy Kintz. Shocking, huh?"

"Not out here," he said. He yanked open the door to the conference room and stood back. Carl wasn't known for holding the door open for women, and I doubted he was starting now. This was to make sure I didn't turn around and run the other way.

I went into the room, and he closed the door behind him. The room was a study in blue and brown. Metal chairs with dark-teal tweed cushions sat around a long fake-wood table. An American flag and the flag of Pennsylvania stood in a grouping in the corner by a wall of floor-to-ceiling bookcases. The shelves were filled with reference material about our city and neighboring towns. I suspected the paper put out the publications to have something more substantial to sell to the public other than the dollar twenty-five daily paper.

"I can explain," I said.

Carl stood by the far side of the room, back-lit by light

filtering through the dingy white horizontal blinds mounted over the window behind him. He was dressed, like he was usually dressed, in a blue-and-white seersucker suit, white shirt, navy-blue tie, and Stan Smith sneakers. His uniform was taken directly from *Kolchak the Night Stalker,* a short-lived TV show from the seventies that ninety percent of the people who encountered Carl had probably never seen.

"I got you this job," he said. "Writing about clothes. That's what you know. How exactly does that qualify you to cover a press conference at the Berks County Correctional Facility for Females?" He scratched his head. "It makes no sense. They're not fashionable. They wear orange jumpsuits."

"They wear gray sweats," I said. Carl glared at me. "Khaki when they're on work detail."

"You're kidding."

"I know! I expected them to be in orange too."

He waved his hand. "I'm not talking about their clothes. You went to the press conference and came away with a story about what they were wearing? This is unbelievable. You didn't even take notes, did you?"

I chose not to bring up my Barbie notebook. "No," I said.

"It gets better every minute. A monthly columnist gets *my* invitation to the press conference of the year and forgets to take notes. Kidd, I don't know how you've made it this far, because you are too stupid to live."

I slammed my palms down on the table. "Hey!" I proclaimed. "Will you shut up?" He did, to his credit, remain silent. "I wasn't at the press conference. I was *inside* the prison. Meeting with Suzy Kintz herself."

"Nice try."

I pulled Joey Carducci's card out from my pocket. "Don't believe me? Call Joey Carducci at the *Philadelphia Post*. He was there when they called my name and led me inside. He wanted me to say he was my assistant so he could come with me, but I told him I wanted the scoop for the *Eagle*."

Carl took the card and pulled out his cell phone. He held the card up in his left hand and dialed with the thumb on his right. "Carducci? This is Carl Collins from the *Ribbon* — yeah. That's right." Carl lowered the card and watched me while he spoke. His expression changed, less angry and more relaxed. "Yeah, she's here with me now. Uh-huh. She told me she said that. You get a good story?" He paused. "We're working on something a little different than that. Sure. Thanks." He hung up and lowered his phone.

He turned around and peered between the blinds and then turned back to face me. He owed me an apology, and I knew that would be hard for Carl. I crossed my arms and raised my eyebrows, waiting for him to say something.

"Okay. I'll share a by-line with you, but that's it."

"You're kidding," I said, this time parroting him. I added, "Carl, I didn't go there to steal your story. I didn't even know there was a press conference. Suzy's lawyer arranged for me to visit with her. Suzy and I went to high school together. She read your profile of me in the paper and wants me to help her with the documentation she needs to apply for a retrial."

"You mean this wasn't a one-time thing?"

"Not if I don't want it to be."

Carl pulled out a chair and sat down. He stared at the books on the shelf, but his eyes were unfocused, like he wasn't seeing them, but rather something in his mind. "What do you know about her case?"

"Nothing. I didn't even live in Pennsylvania when she was arrested."

"There was a boycott of Kintz pretzels that spiked the sales of the other pretzels by default," he said. "Some grocery stores found the Kintz pretzel bags torn open on the shelves so when people picked them up, they spilled out on the floor. I worked in the mail room. We were inundated with letters to the editor. Half the town wanted to know what was going to happen to her, and the other half threatened to cancel their subscriptions if we didn't kill the story."

"Which way did you go?"

"If it had been me, I would have kept writing the story. Scandal sells papers. But once she was arrested, the editor at the time told us to move on to something else."

"And what happened to Suzy?"

"She sat in the county jail until her trial, but when she was convicted and sentenced to prison for life, it all went away. Almost like once she was out of the county, she was out of everybody's mind."

"She's in the Berks County Correctional Facility," I said.

"She wasn't always. After her arrest, she was held in a local jail for two years, awaiting trial. After the conviction, she went to a maximum-security prison in Muncy."

"Where's that?"

"About two hours north. It's where they send adult

female offenders. She was expected to remain there until she died."

"Then why was she moved to the Berks County Correctional Facility?"

"Her mother got sick a couple of years ago. Suzy petitioned the courts to move her closer so visits wouldn't tax the family as much."

"You know a lot about this case," I said.

"I'm a reporter."

"You said you worked in the mailroom, so you weren't a reporter when this happened. You're close to my age, aren't you?"

"Close, yeah. When I was looking for a job, I wrote a handful of sample articles to indicate what I was capable of. One them was about Suzy Kintz."

"Do you still have it?"

"It's at home somewhere," he said. "That was years ago. Besides, it was mostly conjecture. I was a kid reporter trying to pad his resume with articles written on spec. All of the facts came from news that had already been published."

So she'd been moved. It was probably nothing, just a routine decision by the powers that be, but it seemed there were a lot of little nothings about Suzy's case that I should know before talking to her again.

Suzy's arrest took place while I was on a buying trip. When I returned home to my apartment in New York, I lived my life. It wasn't until Christmas, over eggnog and Unique Splits Extra Dark pretzels, that my mom asked if I'd heard the news. The details shared were vague, the subject dropped, and that had been that.

Until today. Sure, getting a letter from her attorney set

the ball in motion, but sitting across from her in the visiting area of the prison had made it all real.

It also made it on her terms. Everything she'd told me, everything I knew, it all hinged on one fact: I'd known her before any of this happened. The opinion I'd formed of Suzy Kintz had been shaped in the hallways of Ribbon High School. Before I stepped foot inside that depressing concrete building today, my expectations were in line with the past, not the present. That might work for Suzy — it might be exactly what she wanted — but it didn't work for me. It felt, I hated to admit, like I was being manipulated.

"I'd like to know more about the case before I decide what to do," I said to Carl.

"What's to decide? You're going back and getting an exclusive. I'd come with you, but unless you convince Kintz to approve me as a visitor, the best I'll get is an interview with the staff. If you don't want to write it, I will. You can be my source."

I held up my hand. "Don't count on your Pulitzer just yet. I haven't agreed to anything. Suzy Kintz is someone I knew a long time ago, but it's not like we were friends. I barely knew her. She said she's innocent, but I don't even know if I believe her."

Carl's face colored red. "She wants your help. That's what you do, right? That's how you get mixed up in these things. You try to solve other people's problems, and it's almost gotten you killed a couple of times. I know you're going to do this, Kidd. I wrote the article that put you on the map. What do you need to know before you say yes?"

"Get me access to the archives. Wendy says you're the

only one who ever goes there. I need to see how well her story lines up with what the press reported."

Carl jumped up and pushed his chair back under the table. "Let's go."

I felt a familiar tingling sensation, the excitement that comes from discovering something new. Since the holidays, I'd been going through the motions of life. Money had simplified a lot of things, but writing a style column for the paper wasn't my life's work. It was a placeholder that kept me busy while I figured out my next move. I'd thought — we all thought — that working for the paper would be safe and steady and keep me from trouble.

I followed Carl out of the conference room, down the hall past cubicles of writers and past the break room where vending machines and burnt coffee kept the staff fueled on junk food and caffeine. Carl went to his desk and pulled a roll of cherry-flavored Tums out of his drawer. He unpeeled the roll and popped two in his mouth while we walked, then dropped the roll into his jacket pocket.

He turned to me and said, "We'll take the stairs down. It's faster." His breath smelled like Swedish Fish.

Carl knew his way around the newspaper offices, and his shortcut delivered us two floors down by a dimly lit desk and a closed metal door. An older man in a faded blue button-down shirt and jeans sat with his feet up on the desk, reading a John Updike novel. At the sound of us approaching he lowered his feet and put the book in a drawer, but then, when he recognized Carl, he relaxed. "Oh. It's you." He pulled the book back out and set it on his desktop.

"Andy, this is Samantha Kidd. She's working with me

on a story." He glanced at me with a look that said now might not be the time to disagree. I forced a smile which seemed to appease him. "She's going to spend some time in the archives. Get her what she needs, okay?"

"Sure," Andy said.

Carl stepped back. "I'll be at my desk. Come see me when you're done." He left the way we came.

Andy stood up and pulled a ring of keys from his desk. "What'cha looking for?" he asked. "Must be local history. Everything recent is online."

I stuck with the local-history angle and gave Andy the year I wanted to see. He pulled a large binder, the size of a newspaper, from the shelf with some effort and set it on the table in the middle of the room. "You got gloves?"

"No."

"Here." He held a pair of small white gloves out to me. "Finger oils are the devil. These materials are fragile, and when they're gone, they're gone."

I thanked him, and he left. When the door behind him was shut, I lifted the thick metal cover to the binder. Inside were daily newspapers for the month of November, from the year the crime had taken place. I flipped half of the papers forward and then went page by page, seeking the headline that told me I was on the right date.

The article I sought was on the last Friday of the month. The article was buried on page four in the "Crime in Berks County" page of the Times. Among other reports of police activity was a summary of the crime.

At two a.m. police responded to a 911 call from the Kintz guest cottage. Responding officers found a man fatally wounded upon arrival. The victim's wife, who made the 911 call, was the only person present at the scene. She was questioned on site and taken into custody. The residents were asleep in the main house and were unaware that a crime had been committed on their property.

The story was vague. As if the reporters went out of their way not to mention Suzy, or to link her to the Kintz family by mentioning her relationship to them. I flipped to the Saturday paper. It was the last one in the binder, and there was no mention of the crime.

CHAPTER 10
A Big Deal

I CLOSED THE LARGE BINDER AND SNEEZED. DUST particles swarmed around me. I sneezed again. The third time, the door opened and Andy came in. "You okay?" he asked.

"I'm fine," I said. "The dust got up my nose."

He grunted. "Don't be sneezing on the archives." He looked down at the binder. "You find what you need?"

I glanced down at the binders. "I'm doing some initial recon. Figuring out what it is I need."

"What are you looking for?"

I hesitated for a moment, and then went for it. "I'm looking for articles on the Trenton Vega murder case. So far all I've found is a four-inch summary buried on the local crime page."

"So?"

"So, it was a big deal. A murder. The suspect went to Ribbon High School, and her family owns one of the lynchpin pretzel companies."

"The victim was a New Yorker. The suspect may have grown up here, but it wasn't a 'local girl done good' story. We dropped the story shortly after the arrest."

I sat up a little straighter. "Why?"

"Subscribers threatened to cancel their subscriptions if the reporters continued reporting on it. A lot of people thought the paper glamorized it so they could get national attention."

"How do you glamorize a double homicide?" I asked, not expecting Andy to answer. I glanced at his faded blue button-down shirt and jeans. He wasn't the picture of glamour.

Andy closed the binder I was looking at. He checked the date and then grunted. "Thanksgiving fell on the twenty-eighth that year. The judge didn't sign off on the warrant until Sunday night. We ran the article in Monday's paper. You want the December archives." He looked at his wristwatch. "You got another hour before I secure the room."

That meant it was four. Already today had been long, and I didn't know how much more I could manage without more coffee, but leaving meant having to come back down, and I didn't want to waste time on caffeine consumption.

I thanked Andy, and he left. I located the binder of December archives. Andy might have been right about the initial line item about the crime, but by Monday, it was front page news.

For as light as the first article was on information, this one filled in some gaps. Suzanna Kintz, daughter of pretzel company owners Tom and Katy Kintz, was charged with murdering her husband on Thanksgiving. Evidence at the scene, including the gun that was used in the commission of the crime, indicated a clear-cut case. The judge, who'd been out of town for the holiday weekend, returned Sunday night and signed the warrant before the courts opened on Monday. Suzy had been taken into custody the wee hours of Thanksgiving day and hadn't seen freedom since.

The same timeline that I'd read about in the first article was reprinted here. I copied dates and facts down in my Barbie notepad and then flipped through the binder until I reached the next day. By Tuesday, the story had blossomed. Employees of the restaurant where the group had dined had given quotes about her state of mind hours before the crime. Wednesday, the article contained quotes from board members at the Vega Group, who mourned the loss of their founder. By Thursday, there was no mention of the story at all.

Three days of reporting. Four, if you counted the Local Crime write-up. What should have been a career-making story for a reporter in Ribbon had been summarized into a handful of installments that glossed over the kinds of details people would normally want to read.

I leaned back and considered what the world was like when the crime took place. Shows like CSI hadn't taken over network TV. The closest thing was NYPD Blue, which put the viewer into the mind of the cops and focused on law and order, not on piecing together forensic evidence. I wondered, briefly, how things might be different if a crime like this were committed today. Would the public still threaten to cancel subscriptions, or would a new generation follow every detail and spitball conspiracy theories?

Would the paper even matter when it came to reporting

a story like this? Or had the internet made reporting in print a medium for summarizing a story that was broken online?

I flipped through the rest of the archived copies of the paper in December but found no other mentions of the crime. Carl had said something about Suzy's case — what was it? I pulled out my phone and called him to save time. The screen indicated the call didn't go through.

Andy knocked on the door. "Time to go," he said.

I held up my finger. "One last question. Suzy Kintz sat in a local jail for two years before she was moved to a more permanent location. How can I find that news?"

Andy said, "Yeah, that was two years and change. Coldest winter in years. Figure they wanted her out of here to move her in fifteen-degree temps. Check January. I'll give you five minutes."

I found one small listing two years after her conviction that mentioned her being moved from the local prison to a maximum-security facility in Muncy after her trial. I flipped through binders a month at a time looking for something to indicate when she'd been moved back, but by the time Andy announced my time was up, I'd gotten seven years further and had found nothing.

"I'll help you put these back," he said.

"I'll get them," I said. I stacked one on top of the other and struggled to carry them to the bookcase. "Do I take my gloves or leave them with you?" I asked.

"I'll keep 'em." He held out his hand, and I peeled them off. He pulled an index card out of his drawer and wrote "S. Kidd" on it then folded the card around my gloves and secured the card with a large paperclip. He set them on top of a pile of similarly tagged gloves in a wooden tray on top of a bookcase that sat against the wall.

"You have a system," I said in a friendly tone of voice.

"That's why I'm good at my job," he said. "Not many folks would want to spend their days down here in the dungeon, but I kinda like it. I've got a wife and four daughters at home. No signs of anybody moving out. A man likes his solitude every now and then." He tapped the Updike cover as if Harry Angstrom understood how he felt.

I thanked Andy and took the elevator up to the main floor. (Stairs? In heels? After the day I'd had? No thank you.) The doors opened by the receptionist's desk, but Wendy wasn't there. I returned to the bullpen and debated whether to seek out Carl. Not yet, I decided. I wanted time to process what I knew, what I didn't, and what my next move would be.

———

LATER THAT NIGHT, after dinner of lobster ravioli sauteed in butter with capers and two glasses of chilled white wine, I sat on the sofa with my legs stretched out across Nick's thighs while he massaged my feet. Logan, my faithful black cat, swatted a small felt mouse by Nick's feet. When we both started working from home, we made a pact that dinnertime was sacred, and we stuck to it. (Logan always worked from home, so his agenda didn't need altering.)

Every time I'd offered to help Nick with his sneaker venture, he declined. His father had started the shoe company that he inherited, but Saint Nick was his baby. I knew how much time and energy he was putting into learning about it, sourcing materials, identifying factories, negotiating terms, and making retail connections. And having seen his early prototypes, I knew the collection was good. But as Nick had discovered, the sneaker world was hard to crack. Big companies had endorsement deals with athletes, but designer sneakers didn't compete in that world. It wasn't so much about function as fashion.

Years ago, Nick had scaled back distribution of his shoe collection to open his designer boutiques. It was a sound strategy for a designer who'd had solid double-digit sales growth for ten consecutive years, but it had the side effect of getting his name out of store catalogs and off websites.

It's hard to quantify the effects of that second-hand word of mouth. Nick maybe could have made a go of it with his boutiques, trading off increased exposure for a larger piece of the pie, but when his business got linked to the local mafia, things got difficult. It was in the aftermath that the sneaker idea inspired him, and he'd been so energized by working in a category that was new to him that he hadn't recognized the troubles with him being an unknown.

I'd watched Nick struggle with the challenges of his newest venture, but still, he set it aside at six thirty and gave me his undivided attention. It made me want to find a way to help him even more.

"Hey, Nick? Do I spend a lot of time helping people who don't ask for my help?"

He squeezed the toes on my left foot. "It's part of your charm."

"But if people don't want my help, then doesn't that make doing things for them for me?"

"You lost me."

"I always thought doing things for other people made me generous, but what if what I'm doing for other people isn't what they want me to do? Am I doing that stuff so they'll thank me, or keep me around, or am I doing it because I'm insightful and see what they need that they don't see?"

Nick relaxed his grip on my feet and shifted them from his thighs to the floor. He turned toward me. "Did you have a session with your life coach today?"

"We're on a break," I said. Before he could ask for details, I added, "It was mutual, mostly."

Last year, after acknowledging my attempts to find happiness were met with slammed doors and danger, I sought professional help. At first, the idea of having a sounding board to help parse my forward momentum was a novelty I cherished. But after the money came, the lens through which I viewed happiness shifted. Without the ongoing struggle to make ends meet, I saw, very clearly, that the person standing in the way of my happiness was me.

Somewhere around there was when I decided that true growth meant being uncomfortable. I decided to do the opposite of every instinct that I had. And since having a life coach on which to lean felt comfortable, I did the most uncomfortable thing I could.

I fired her.

(I also paid her a five-thousand-dollar bonus so there would be no hard feelings.)

"Is this about your visit to the correctional facility this morning?" Nick asked.

I tipped my head back and rested it on the sofa cushion

behind me. "It was just like high school," I said like I had told his dad. "She was the aloof girl with the good hair and the calm attitude. I was the nervous one with the coffee stain on my skirt."

"She's the one locked up inside a prison cell and you're the one with your freedom," Nick said gently.

"I know. She was convicted of a horrible crime, and the world thinks she's a dangerous person and should be in prison for life."

"But?"

"But what if she didn't do it?"

"Kidd, did Suzy Kintz tell you why she wanted you to visit with her today?"

"A prisoner in New York confessed to murdering the hiker they found eight miles from the Kintz family compound the day after Trenton Vega was murdered. Suzy was convicted of that crime too, and it's why she was convicted of two life sentences. Now there's a chance that her case will be reviewed. She said she didn't kill her husband. She asked me to find out what I could and decide if I wanted to come back."

"She asked for your help. That should make your decision easier."

"My instincts are to help people when I see they need help. I'm not used to being asked for it."

"Why does that matter? If she didn't do it and she thinks you can help prove it, then how is that different from what you normally do?" He leaned forward and took my face in his hands. "What's bothering you?"

"Her asking me to help is all based on the idea that she

didn't do it." I studied his face and said out loud the one thing that had been troubling me all morning. "But what if she did?"

CHAPTER 11
The Central Question

CUDDLING TURNED INTO ADULT RELATIONS AND WE quickly traded the sofa for the bed. An hour later, I'd forgotten all about Suzy Kintz, and thanks to a maneuver I picked up during a Burlesque-inspired workout video, Nick seemed to have put his business troubles out of his mind too. But in the afterglow, I felt him withdraw to that place of stress that had become his new norm, and despite prompting him to talk about it, he didn't.

The sneaker world is highly competitive and breaking in requires more than a second-generation designer shoe business. Nick's contacts were in Italy, and his client base was moving on to Manolo Blahnik and Jimmy Choo. I wanted to find a way to support him in this new venture, but sneakers weren't my world. If only there were a way to let the world see Nick the way I did, they'd fall in love with him. too. There had to be a way I could help; I just didn't know what it was.

Nick returned to the kitchen to work. I changed into pajamas and turned on the news. Logan hopped onto the sofa and kept me company. The information reported was the same everywhere. The deathbed confession of an inmate in Rikers Prison would likely result in one of Suzy's murder convictions being overturned. To the average viewer, the information meant little. To Suzy, it meant everything.

A life sentence is twenty-five years minimum time served. Suzy's initial sentence of two consecutive life terms meant she'd never see life outside of the prison walls. There was no possibility of parole in the state of Pennsylvania, but Suzy could apply for a new trial or clemency. She'd been a well-behaved prisoner since she'd been locked up. The governor had to at least consider it. This new information was potentially life changing for her.

During a commercial for the latest incontinence drug, I got my notepad and pen. There were too many facts and questions swirling around for me to ignore them, and I didn't want to rely on my memory. Who was the prisoner who'd confessed? Did he have any connection to Suzy, or was this purely coincidence? Who else had been at dinner that night? Where did I need to go to find that information? The questions came at me fast and furious, and after writing them down, I added one more: Who else wanted Trenton Vega dead?

This was the central question to the whole thing. Even Loncar had said it. When a case is closed, the police got their man.

———

THE NEXT MORNING, I woke up with an idea I hadn't considered the day before. I called my friend Eddie Adams, who had the privilege of listening to my craziness both before and after the life coach. He was on a first-name basis with the skeletons in my closet and had also gone to high school with me. Eddie and I hadn't become BFFs until I moved back to Ribbon, but until this morning I'd overlooked him as a source of intel on Suzy.

We met at Benedict's Eggs. Eddie was already seated in the dining room when I slid in opposite him. Today he wore a black T-shirt that said "Tony & Steve & Lance & Mike & Tommy" in white block letters. He leaned back against the booth. A white coffee mug with steam rising off the top sat in front of him. He pulled the mug closer as if he were afraid I'd steal it.

"Hey," he said.

"Hey," I said. Between the two syllables spoken, a world of positive and negative energy passed. I waved to the waiter and pointed to Eddie's mug and then relaxed against the booth. The waiter came by with a mug for me and dropped off two menus. He left us to decide on our meals, and Eddie pulled one menu toward him. I put my hand on top of it so he couldn't open it. "Are you okay?"

"Dude, I am bored. I'm not hardwired to have time off. There's a reason I worked sixty-five hours a week."

"You'll get another job. Just be patient," I said.

"You're the one who has troubled employment history. I'm the reliable one at this table. At least I was." He dropped his head into his hands. His shoulders stood out sharply. "What happened here?" He looked up at me. "Are we in Bizarro World?"

"I resent that."

"I figured you would." He pulled his coffee toward him and drank. I dumped two creamers into mine and stirred.

Until recently, Eddie had been gainfully employed as the visual director for Tradava, a local family-owned retailer. But after a series of financial problems that culminated in the stores being liquidated, Eddie found himself on the wrong side of the steady income equation. He'd saved up enough money to stay afloat and tried to acclimate to a stress-free life outside of retail, but he was wired to have multiple balls in the air, and the peace and quiet made him crazy.

Since then, he picked up freelance work for local businesses. He'd been threatening to move out of Ribbon if he didn't find a job soon, and that meant I'd lose my regular breakfast companion, sometimes chauffeur, and occasional voice of reason. On the heels of firing my life coach, I wasn't willing to lose Eddie's companionship too.

Not telling Eddie about my visit with Suzy had been among the more difficult things in my life, and it was time to spill the beans.

"Do you remember Suzy Kintz?" I asked. "From high school?"

"Sure," he said. "It's crazy that we went to high school with a murderer. I guess there's a reason they tell you to watch out for the silent type."

"I remember her more aloof than silent. She didn't participate. Like she was above it all."

"I had an art class with her. First period. Her paintings were dark."

"Dark how? Her color palette?"

"Yes and no. She painted these giant canvasses. She painted most of the canvas black or dark purple or midnight blue — some goth color — and then added in minute details using a magnifying glass. The details were incredible, but you could barely see them unless you were right on top of the canvas. It was like there was this huge expanse of space and she could focus on a one-inch square. But she never finished them."

"You mean when they were done you thought she could go further?"

The waiter returned to our table, and our conversation was interrupted. Eddie ordered an egg white omelet, protein potatoes, and fresh berries. I went with bacon and French toast. I had a big day ahead of me, and this was my version of power food.

When the waiter left, Eddie answered. "No, I mean she left a chunk of the canvas unpainted. Our teacher told her if she didn't finish at least one, he'd have to give her an incomplete."

"But that means she wouldn't have graduated."

"Yeah, I don't know how she managed that. I saw them having a private meeting one day after school. I was always around the art room those days, and it was during the time the school was investigating the calculus test."

This was a sore spot for Eddie, though it was also the basis for our friendship. Two students had achieved a perfect score on the calculus final. Eddie and the captain of the football team. Not incidentally, they sat next to each other. Suspicion of cheating was immediate.

Eddie had been a new student. An art student. Not expected to excel in math. The football captain had just won our school the district championship. The investigation was a technicality, until I made an appointment with the principal and told him what I'd seen from the back row of the class: that the football captain had copied off Eddie's paper.

The boys were retested separately. Eddie aced the exam. The football captain failed. Eddie kept his scholarship to art school and left Ribbon upon graduation. I didn't know what became of the football captain, but I doubted he'd achieved the professional success Eddie had.

"I was suspended while the principal decided what he was going to do, but Mr. Newman said I could come in before school and get supplies so I could keep painting at home. When I got there, Suzy was in the office with Mr. Newman. One of her canvasses was propped on the desk next to them, and they appeared to be discussing it. When she left, he called me in and asked me what I saw."

"What did you see?"

"I saw what it's like for a person who feels like a tiny part in her world, but who understands there's a lot out there that she has yet to experience. I said it looked to him like she left her paintings unfinished, but to her, that part of the canvas represented how little she felt she knew about life."

Eddie was insightful when it came to art. His natural talent for creation made him excel as a visual director, and he'd once had the chance to curate an exhibit at the local museum. It didn't surprise me that he and his teacher had discussed another student's work, nor that he'd been able to see something the teacher had not.

"What happened after that? I mean, she graduated, so

he must have changed his mind, but did anything come of it?"

"She talked to me at graduation. Our teacher told her what I said about her work. She said I saw through her. She said she painted her feelings, but she always figured if she kept the paintings abstract nobody would know what was going on inside her head."

"That's a compliment, right?"

"Hard to say. An artist paints for him or herself. If someone is tortured, it's an outlet."

"Like therapy?"

"No, like an exorcism. A way to temporarily release the turmoil. The emotions, chaos, whatever you want to call it are inside the painting for interpretation by anyone who looks at it, but it's not the artist's job to explain things. I got the feeling painting liberated her from something she wanted to escape. I don't know if she kept up with it after high school. Maybe if she had, none of this would have happened."

CHAPTER 12
Dude. Deets. Now

THERE WAS NO SENSE KEEPING MY SECRET ANY LONGER. "I saw her yesterday," I said. "Suzy Kintz. At the correctional facility. She made arrangements through her lawyer for me to visit."

Eddie didn't react at first. He kept his eyes on mine, and I waited for him to say something. I braced myself for the initial *how could you not tell me?* or the less expected but possibly also fitting *does Nick know?*, neither of which came. Our food did, interrupting the silence and giving us both something to focus on other than the conversation.

The longer Eddie went without saying anything, the more concerned I got. It wasn't like him to be offended at something I did, and we were good enough friends that he didn't pull punches when it came to giving me advice. The silent treatment was new.

I sliced into my French toast and speared a corner of the battered and syrupy slice of bread. Before putting it into my mouth, I asked, "Are you mad?"

"Eat your food before it gets cold," he said with a mouth full of berries.

I waited a few seconds and then put the toast in my mouth. They'd used thick slices of bread, and the sugar and maple syrup, combined with the batter and butter, kept me from being able to speak further. I chewed and swallowed and repeated, and almost forgot about Eddie's unusual silence when he spoke.

"You went to the correctional facility to visit a murderer who we went to high school with and *didn't think to tell me?*"

I choked on the mouthful of French toast and reached for my water glass to wash it down. Eddie pulled my glass out of reach. I put my hand to my throat and stifled a cough. He pushed the glass toward me, and I emptied half of it while my eyes watered.

"Geez!" I said after I swallowed. "Passive aggressive much?"

"Dude. Deets. Now."

I pointed the tines of my fork at my plate. "But my food will get cold."

"Your arteries will thank you later."

I set my utensils down and drank some coffee then told Eddie how my visit with Suzy had come about. "The invitation came to the newspaper. I had to make copies of my identification and have a background check done, and then I was told to go yesterday morning at nine o'clock."

"Is that why she's all over the news?"

"There was a press conference. I didn't know that at the time, but one of the other reporters asked which outlet I was with, and when I said the *Ribbon Eagle*, he treated me like I was a reporter just like the rest of the crowd. Like I belonged. I assumed there had been a mistake and sat down, and then the prison director called my name and told me to go inside."

By now, Eddie had forgotten all about his breakfast. He dropped his fork, and a red raspberry rolled off his plate and onto the table. It landed by a white napkin and stained the corner red.

"While the press pool of Pennsylvania was sitting outside getting information from the prison warden, you were inside talking one on one with Suzy?"

"Yes."

"Did you get strip searched?"

"Don't be silly," I said and then added, "I got patted down."

He shook his head and smiled. "I always knew you'd see the inside of a prison."

I threw my napkin at him. He caught it, set it on the table on top of the raspberry, and leaned back. "What was she like?"

"She was the same. There she was, in prison clothes like everybody else, but she looked like she was born to wear them. Her hair was shiny and brown, and her skin was perfect. She shouldn't have looked as good as she looked, not after spending seventeen years inside a jail cell. Aside from some extra weight, she was the same Suzy Kintz from high school." I waited a moment while that sank in. "It doesn't seem possible. How could that be possible? How could she be unchanged?"

"Why are you changed?" Eddie asked.

"Me? I've been changed by life. Living in New York

and then moving back here. Job after job after job, being almost killed a couple of times, getting married. Going from being broke to having money."

"Okay, now think about Suzy. Her family is rich, so she's never had to stress about money, and she was arrested when she was twenty-two."

"But she killed someone."

"So people say."

"You think she's innocent?"

"Dude, if you thought she was guilty, would you have gone to visit her yesterday?"

I sat back. Eddie had a way of cutting through the crap, and this time he'd landed on the hundred-thousand-dollar question. Suzy had been convicted of two murders. That made her a dangerous and unstable person. Why had I gone so willingly? I kept asking what if she were guilty? But the true question, the one that kept me awake last night, was this: what if she were innocent?

We paid for our breakfasts and left. A copy of the *Philadelphia Post* sat on a leather bunker inside the restaurant. I picked up the paper and unfolded it to expose the article above the fold on the front page. The headline proclaimed, "New Twist in Pretzel Heiress Murder Case." The reporter was Joey Carducci.

I felt a rush of adrenaline. The *Ribbon Eagle* might have backed off the story, but the *Post* likely did not. I tucked the paper under my arm and followed Eddie to the parking lot. I promised to keep him filled in on anything Suzy Kintz-related, and we went to our individual cars.

After Eddie drove off, I unfolded the newspaper and scanned the article. It contained a recap of the information delivered by the warden yesterday along with a rehash of the evidence that led to Suzy's conviction. But what struck me about the article wasn't Joey's coverage of the press conference (which was thorough; I'd give him that), but the sentence under the headline that indicated this was the first in a series that covered the unfolding story of Suzy Kintz's request for clemency.

I read the article, looking for something I didn't know. This would be just one of a hundred articles about the press conference yesterday. The one paper that didn't have a scoop was mine, because I hadn't been in the audience. For all the inside information I'd received, I hadn't heard what the other reporters had, and it struck me as an oversight that no one else at my paper had known about the event. Why hadn't the crime reporter of the media in Suzy's hometown been notified?

I scanned the article again. It was the same information I'd heard while watching the news with Nick last night. New evidence to exonerate Suzy from the second murder that had led to her double life sentence. No comment yet from the governor's office. Come back tomorrow for more details.

I reached into my handbag and pulled out Joey's card. I could call him and ask what I'd missed, but he'd expect something in return. I set Joey's card down and looked up the number for the governor's office. I didn't expect to get a direct line, but I couldn't do nothing. I called the number and, when a man answered, introduced myself.

"This is Samantha Kidd from the *Ribbon Eagle*. I'm calling to get a statement on the Suzy Kintz case from the governor's office."

"Hold please," he said. A few moments later, the man returned. "We've been inundated with calls about this. The governor prepared a statement for the press. We released it this morning. Did you not get it?"

"Our servers are down," I lied. "Can you read it to me?"

"Sure. Tell me when you're ready."

"I'm ready."

"Okay. 'Thank you for your interest in the Pennsylvania legal system. We have reviewed the new evidence in the Vega murder case, and while it seemed compelling at first, we have concluded it to be unreliable. Suzy Kintz's original conviction stands. Any further questions should be directed to the governor's press office.' Do you need me to repeat it?"

I'd never been great at dictation but had stopped writing around the word "unreliable." "The governor has already made a decision?" I asked. "Suzy couldn't have petitioned for clemency already."

"She doesn't have to. That entitled rich girl can buy as many deathbed confessions as she wants. It doesn't matter what new evidence comes to light."

"I thought the legal system was supposed to be unbiased."

"That's the media. The legal system is supposed to determine the truth."

"It doesn't sound like you're even looking."

"We have the truth. The police did their job, and the conviction stands. Suzy Kintz is never getting out."

CHAPTER 13

Partners

I DON'T DO WELL WITH ABSOLUTES. WORDS LIKE "never" are like a shiny object: *pay attention to me!* And if the governor's office was digging in their heels twenty-four hours after new evidence came to light in a seventeen-year-old murder case, then there was more to this story. I wasn't ready to tip my hand just yet, so I thanked the man from the governor's office and hung up and stared out my window at nothing in particular while I considered my options.

I could go in to the paper and look at the archives again. Maybe I'd missed something yesterday.

But there was a note of familiarity to what the governor's office said, and it took me a moment to recall why. Detective Loncar had intimated the same thing. If the case was closed, then the guilty party was in jail.

Loncar's retirement came after decades of work on the police force. He'd moved to Ribbon from Harrisburg, because a case had let him see that bad things happened in small towns as much as they happened in big cities, and working in Ribbon meant he could make a difference. That meant he wasn't part of the investigation that ultimately put Suzy in prison. He'd dismissed me yesterday when I was still dealing in vague details. I wondered if today, after seeing the news and reading the papers, he'd feel differently about my questions.

I drove back to his office. The lot was near empty, with the highest congestion of cars parked around the liquor store. It was ten thirty in the morning. Make of that what you will.

Today, Geri Loncar, the detective's daughter and some-times receptionist, sat at the desk outside the detective's office. His door was closed. She smiled broadly and held her index finger up to her lips, and then pointed at a portable crib that sat in the corner behind her. A small baby in a white cotton onesie slept with his hands in little fists by the sides of his head.

I stared at the small baby and then looked back at Geri. "Yours?" I mouthed.

She nodded. "I didn't know I was pregnant! Can you believe it? You hear about stuff like that, but you don't believe it until it happens to you."

"You mean you went nine months and had no idea?"

She laughed. "I'm not that out of touch with my body. I mean, I've been seeing someone, but we weren't trying. It just happened. I didn't have morning sickness or pregnancy cravings or anything this time. And he *sleeps*. He's nothing like my first baby."

I pointed my thumb at Loncar's office. "Your dad is okay with you bringing the baby to the office?"

"I don't think it would have been his first choice, but he needed someone to cover the phones today, and it was short notice." She glanced at his closed door and then back to me. "You sure you don't want the job?"

"We work better as partners," I said.

I'd wondered, more than once, why Loncar hadn't found a more permanent solution to his receptionist problem. He was a more than competent investigator, but he never seemed to be inundated by work. I'd joked about his cases being of the cheating-husband variety, though it was entirely possible that I'd hit the nail on the head.

Since Loncar was behind closed doors, I went to the crib and peered in at the sleeping baby. The subject of starting a family with Nick had come up more than once, and I'd even thought, for a brief moment, that I was pregnant. But still, the idea of being responsible for a tiny little life was something I hadn't been able to wrap my head around, and with the exception of Logan, my cat, and Bardot, Nick's dad's French bulldog, I sometimes thought it was a marvel that I'd managed to take care of myself all these years.

After ogling the baby, I readdressed Geri. "Is someone in there with him?"

"A potential client." She dropped her voice. "I can tell you. You're practically family. Conrad Vega is on the other side of that door. The media is stirring up details about his son's murder case, and he wants a professional to make sure they don't slur the family name."

"Do you know anything about the case?" I asked. "Did you follow it when it happened?"

"Are you kidding? I was glued to the TV. She was the ultimate bad girl. They called her 'Boozy Suzy' because she could hold her liquor." She lowered her voice to a whisper. "Did you know she made a sex tape?"

"I heard it was a porno."

Geri rolled her eyes. "Nothing that sordid. It was her and her husband on a yacht by the south of France."

"Did you see it?"

She shook her head. "No, but I heard it was classy. Dad caught me telling my friends I wanted to be like her. He said if he ever caught me idolizing a murderer again, I'd be grounded for life."

I straightened up and looked at the closed door. "You said Trenton Vega's dad is in there?"

"Yep. Good thing, too. Dad can use a client like him."

The implications of Loncar taking this case hit me like a punch to the gut. If I helped Suzy, then Loncar would likely be my opponent. There would be no mentor/mentee conversations or friendly advice. One of us would be right and the other would be wrong. It wouldn't be like when he worked for the police department and I was little more to him than a nuisance in a well-coordinated outfit.

I was torn between leaving before Loncar knew I'd been there or staying to see what I might find out. Being practically family and all, the odds of getting information from Geri — at least as long as the door remained closed — were in my favor. The decision was made for me when the door opened and Loncar's appointment stepped out.

The man could have been in his nineties, but his choice in clothes indicated he hadn't given up on the good life. He wore a white oxford under a camel vest and a camel-and-amber plaid blazer, over straight-legged jeans that were faded in all the right places. Expensive Italian loafers,

Cartier tank watch, and a modest gold wedding band completed his look. He must have really been something in his day.

"I'll be in touch," Loncar said to him, breaking the tension. I turned my back on the men and heard the bells chime over the door while a cool breeze teased my neck, and then the door dropped back into place.

"Ms. Kidd," Loncar said.

I turned around. "Detective," I answered. "New partner?" I asked, tipping my head toward the door.

He crossed his arms. "Did we have an appointment?"

"Nope. Just dropped by to say hi to Geri." I turned to Geri and smiled.

She looked confused. "How did you know I would be here?" she asked.

"Yes, Ms. Kidd, how did you know my daughter would be here?"

Think fast, Samantha! "I was in the area and I spotted her car." I pointed out at an orange Kia Soul. I'd borrowed her car around Christmas, and now whenever I saw an orange car, I thought of her. Turns out there are a lot of orange cars on the road.

Loncar walked to the door and held it open. "And what are you driving these days?"

There were less than a dozen cars in the entire parking lot, and there seemed no point trying to avoid the question. "The silver Nissan Leaf," I said.

"You drive an electric car?" Geri asked. "I'd be afraid the battery would die while I was out."

"That hardly ever happens," I said. I turned to Loncar.

Loncar walked out of the office toward my car. I said a

hasty goodbye to Geri and ran after him. What was he going to do? Break a taillight so it would be easier to follow me at night?

I caught up to him by the license plate. "It's on loan from the dealer," I said. "They've been very understanding about my vehicular indecision."

"Tanner Auto," Loncar said.

"Yes."

"Out on Pottsville Pike?"

"Yes. Why? Are you ready to trade in the dark gray beater you drive?" I glanced to my left and right and found Loncar's nondescript car parked by the end of the lot. "Tanner Auto has a sweet GR Supra A91 Edition in Refraction blue in their showroom. It would spruce up your image."

He ignored my suggestion. "You think you'll stick with the Nissan?"

Not a chance. "Maybe," I said. "I'll probably drive it around for a few more days, maybe a week or two. If you see me, be sure to wave!" I aimed my remote at the car and unlocked it and then climbed in and shut the door. Loncar stood to the side, watching me. I started the engine and backed out of the lot then headed directly to Tanner Auto to trade the Nissan in for something a little less noticeable.

CHAPTER 14
Pretzel Boycott

MY TRANSACTION AT TANNER AUTO WAS QUICK AND painless. Ian Tanner was on a conference call, but Kent spotted me and processed the paperwork required to swap the silver Nissan Leaf out for an electric Volvo XC40 Recharge SUV. The decision had been easy; it was the least Nissan-like car on the lot.

"This one just came back yesterday and hasn't been fully charged," Kent said.

"I'll plug it in when I get home," I promised. I collected the keys and left.

As I drove, I found my thoughts returning to Suzy's situation. At my visit yesterday, she said she wanted me to know the facts as they'd been reported before we discussed anything further. After a minimal effort spent, I still didn't know the facts. I didn't know much of anything. But I knew that I wanted to know more, and that, for now, was enough.

Writing the column for the *Ribbon Eagle* gave me a certain amount of autonomy. They expected me to find myself in unique situations where I could talk about local style, but the truth was, more people seemed interested in where I went than what I wore. It wasn't the outlandish destinations that captivated their attention either, it was the regional ones that defined our town. There were more letters to the editor after I attended the local Chili Pepper Festival than when I went up in a hot air balloon in Chester County.

Later today, my editor, Monty, expected the pitch for my next "Style on the Street" column. Now that I knew Suzy's case would gain national attention, putting forth details of my visits seemed a poor idea. There had to be a way to leverage this.

I drove back into town. Traffic, which should have been nonexistent at this time, was sluggish. I turned off the main road and took residential streets. I knew this area well; in a few miles, I'd come out at a light by the soft pretzel store. I might as well pick up a couple dozen for the office.

But the traffic jam hadn't come from an accident. It came from the parking lot to the pretzel store. Cars spilled out onto the street, waiting for spaces to open. I'd never seen them so busy. Were they giving away free pretzels or something?

It was twenty minutes before I was parked and inside. Instead of the college-aged employees who knew me by sight, the owner was behind the counter. "What can I get you today?"

"I'll take three dozen," I ordered.

"We're fresh out," he said. He pointed to the giant pretzel oven. "It'll be a couple of minutes."

"I'll wait," I said. He rung up the sale, and when there

appeared to be no discount, I asked the obvious question. "What's with the crowd?"

"Pretzel boycott," he said. "When I saw the news, I figured it was going to be busy today. Had to cancel my golf game."

"Pretzel boycott?" I repeated. This was new, and as a lifelong fan of the pretzel, it seemed like something I would have been exposed to by now.

"Yeah. You know Kintz pretzels?" he asked.

I nodded.

"One of the kids got into trouble a while back. Convicted of killing a couple of people. The family tried to shut down the story, but a death row inmate in New Jersey confessed to the murders so it's in the news again."

I didn't bother correcting the man on the various details he'd gotten wrong from the story. To do so would have been to tip my hand on how much I knew, and what mattered was that the press conference and subsequent news had mobilized the community.

"You said you expected it to be busy today?"

"Yep. The *Philadelphia Post* called me for a quote for a series of articles they're writing. Good thing I answered the call. We've already tripled our sales."

He left me at the counter and retrieved my three dozen pretzels. I left, making room for the next person in line. The pretzels were too hot to eat, but that didn't stop me from burning my mouth anyway. There were few things in life as satisfying as the twist in a fresh, hot soft pretzel. Besides, a burned mouth was the perfect excuse for ice cream later today.

Curiosity led me not to the paper, but to Kintz Pretzels.

Unlike the soft pretzel store where I'd just been, the lot appeared empty. A woman stood on the patch of grass in front of the building, holding a sign that said, "Believe in justice? Boycott Kintz Pretzels."

I turned a hard left, and the bag of pretzels slipped from the passenger seat onto the floor and landed on top of the newspaper I'd taken from the restaurant that morning. Joey Carducci's headline stared at me. "First in a series" implied he was planning on saying more on the matter.

I parked outside Kintz Pretzels and pulled the paper toward me. Joey's article summarized the details I already knew from the news last night: an inmate's confession to murder altered the facts in the case against Suzy. She should be entitled to a new trial. At best, she should be eligible for clemency. At worst, her sentence should be reduced to one life term. The governor's office made it seem as though neither option would be considered. They felt confident she was a murderer and belonged behind bars.

But what if?

What if Suzy hadn't killed Trenton Vega? Then someone else had. It was the fact that no one was talking about. That a different crime with a different killer might have taken place that night, a crime that had nothing to do with the pretzel heiress who'd spent almost half of her life in jail. A killer whose freedom would be threatened by a new investigation into what happened that night.

I pulled out Joey Carducci's card and stared at the number for a few seconds before making up my mind. I called his cell, and he answered halfway through the first ring.

"Carducci."

"Joey, this is Samantha Kidd. We met outside the Berks County Correctional Facility for Females." There really did need to be a shorter way to say that.

"I remember. You went inside while the rest of us got the sanitized version. I was looking forward to reading your story. Is your paper holding it for the weekend?"

"Not exactly." I hadn't made this call to pussyfoot around the conversation. "Here's the deal. Suzy arranged for me to visit her. I had no idea about the press conference or the confession from the prisoner at Rikers. And now I'm trying to piece some background together, but I'm not having any luck."

"Read your archives."

"I was hoping you would send over what you have."

"You're kidding, right? You don't know how journalism works, do you?"

"Sure, I do. I've seen *All the President's Men*."

Joey was silent for a few beats. "On one condition. Your subscriber base might not care about this story, but mine does. I get exclusive rights to your conversations with Suzy from prison."

"I can't agree to that. I'll lose all credibility as a journalist."

Joey went silent again. Considering my last column was about yoga pants, it's possibly I overplayed the journalist card.

"It was one visit," I added. I briefly replayed the highlight reel from my time with Suzy. "We talked about me, mostly."

"When are you going to visit her again?"

I didn't know. I'd pretended that it was a one-time thing,

but I knew all along that it wasn't. "Send a copy of your archives to my attention at the *Ribbon Eagle*. I'll make the arrangements."

"This isn't the olden days, Kidd. I'll email you a zip file."

"Oh. Yes. Right. I'll be in touch."

We hung up. I called Suzy's attorney and arranged to visit her again. This time, I'd be more prepared.

CHAPTER 15

Fresh Content

I DROVE TO THE PAPER. TODAY WENDY, THE receptionist, was dressed in a red, white, and blue flowered shirt over jeans. A pink, green, and white floral scarf was knotted around her neck. Last month I'd submitted an article about not being afraid to mix and match prints, and seeing her interpretation of that article was a strong case for writing about neutrals. She was on a call but held her free hand up and sat back so I could see her sweater. I gave her a thumbs up, forced a smile, and went inside to my cubicle.

The *Ribbon Eagle* had gone through multiple permutations since its inception. Decades ago, there had been both morning and afternoon editions, the morning called "the Eagle" and the afternoon called "the Times." As the subscriber base shrank, the paper was forced to choose between the two. Their first choice, the afternoon edition, was a disaster. It turned out people like getting a morning paper to read with their coffee, and cancellations flooded the front desk. A quick adjustment (and rehire of all of the delivery boys who'd had to quit due to scheduling conflicts with after-school activities) was effected. The easiest way to communicate that the morning paper was back was to revert to the old paper name, and so, the *Ribbon Eagle/Times* turned *Ribbon Times* was now the *Ribbon Eagle*.

Some days, the local news is exhausting.

These days, the most important thing the paper needed was fresh content. Our layout team had been replaced with a college student who arranged articles digitally like a tangram, minimizing page count and print costs. Most subscribers received both the digital and print copies, but the open rates on our emails was low enough to indicate people still wanted good old-fashioned newsprint.

I checked my email and, not finding anything from Joey, started work on my pitch for Monty. My columns had a format to them. I started with the assignment, then the dress code. Next came a detailed description of my outfit, and finally, a couple of paragraphs that outlined the event in question. It begged for a photo, but Monty said the column wasn't popular enough to give up for that, so I got the Dear Abby treatment with a selfie. (I would have preferred a sketch.)

I finished my pitch and sent it to my editor. I checked my email – still nothing from Joey – hit refresh and double-checked the spam folder too. I considered a few opening sentences about pretzel style when a gruff voice barked my name from somewhere behind me.

"Kidd," Monty called. It sounded like a warning shot fired over the heads of the bullpen. He was rarely seen in the open during the day. Disciplinary conversations took place in his office. But when he did come out to talk to someone, it meant he wanted the rest of the staff to hear, and it appeared as though today was my lucky day.

He strode toward me and waved my email. "You're supposed to go to events around Ribbon and write about them using your unique background as the hook. Our subscribers like to read about our town. Without the event, all you're doing is writing a fashion column. We're not that kind of paper."

"You could be," I said. "I can't be the only person in Ribbon who likes clothes."

"Collins says you were at the local correctional facility yesterday," he said. "Is that true?"

"Yes."

"But you didn't cover the press conference."

"No. I didn't know about the press conference when I went," I said. "Suzy Kintz used to sit behind me in homeroom. She read Carl's profile on me. I guess they get the paper in jail. You should tell circulation."

He tossed a printout of my email onto my desk. The word "prison" was written in red ink and circled several times. "Forget pretzel fashion. The prison's your story. You're on special assignment. I want five hundred words about the correctional facility."

"The dress code for prison visits is available on their website," I said. "Why would we reprint it here?"

"I want the story. Five hundred words about your visit with Kintz. Throw in the dress code details if you want. Have it to me by the end of the day."

"But my column doesn't run for two more weeks!"

"You're getting the sidebar on the front page. Scandal is

good for business, Kidd. Let's not let the *Philadelphia Post* get all the credit."

I considered negotiating for a better photo while Monty returned to his office. Rumors about how he spent his days in there abounded, but until now, my role at the paper had been so minor that I hadn't cared. He could be playing internet card games, and it wouldn't bother me.

I started a new document and followed my template. After copying and pasting the dress code into my file and describing my pink jersey outfit (I left out the coffee stain), I collected my thoughts about what to write. The more I thought about the visit, the more I reflected on what Suzy had told me about that night. It was human nature to want to gain sympathy from your audience, and if I was Suzy's audience of one, then it was to be expected that she'd tailor her story to me. I hadn't had the privilege of boning up on her background before our visit like she had. It bothered me in an unexplainable way that she knew about my crime-solving reputation. Like she had an edge over me.

I typed up details from memory, but my writing lacked spark. It still felt precious, like a memory I wanted to protect. A real reporter, like Joey or Carl, would exploit it. They would leverage the story about Suzy lighting one cigarette to either indicate the peace she'd made with her circumstances or illustrate the inner belief system that allowed her to commit murder without remorse. They would compare and contrast the memories of the person they knew in high school to the person in front of them and provide the world a window to what seventeen years of incarceration did to a person's spirit.

They would not talk about memories of eyeshadow application.

My editor wanted a "Style on the Street" column that he could use to sell papers, but that wasn't what could make this article special. It was what I knew about Suzy that they didn't. What I remembered from high school.

Suzy had sat behind me in homeroom, and she often entered the room and took her seat just as the bell rang. She carried a rose-gold backpack from class to class. One time, out of curiosity, I followed her to her locker and made an excuse to talk to a classmate in the halls so I could see inside when she opened it. Every one of my classmates had decorated their lockers with magazine clippings and photos, some with the occasional birthday card or love note. Suzy's had nothing but a stack of books. For the two and a half years we attended Ribbon High together, she showed no interest in being part of the crowd.

There were two types of disinterested students in high school. Those who were already beyond the lesson plan, and those who were going through the motions until they got their diplomas. By senior year, Suzy's too-cool-for-school routine had convinced me, and everyone else, that she was the latter. She had a pretzel fortune waiting for her when she graduated. High school was a way to pass the time until she joined the company business.

But one day after school, halfway home, I realized I'd forgotten my French homework. I returned to the school and parked in a lot that was empty save for faculty and one recognizable car: Suzy's white convertible. Had she done something to get her detention? Or more sensational: was she having an affair with a teacher?

I could still feel the nervous excitement I felt that day when I went back into the school. I was aware of every sound, smell, and noise. I wanted to discover something nobody else knew.

I walked through the halls and overheard two female voices conversing in fluent French. This was not the tentative dialect of classmates sounding out words phonetically. These were people who'd been speaking French their whole lives.

I reached the room and paused outside the door. I could stand out here and listen for hours, but I'd never know what they said because I was still learning how to conjugate a verb. But I needed that assignment, and there was no point eavesdropping on a conversation that was over my head.

When I entered the room, I found my teacher sitting at her desk and Suzy in a chair opposite. They both turned and looked at me. My teacher looked surprised; Suzy, curious.

"I forgot my homework," I said.

"*En Francais,*" my teacher said. (She insisted we speak French – or try to – during class, which led to a lot of people introducing themselves to each other and a couple of guys quoting lyrics from "Lady Marmalade.")

"*J'ai voudrais un . . .* homework," I said.

My teacher laughed. Suzy said, "Dev-*wuah.*"

"Dev-*wuah,*" I repeated. She nodded. I said it a few times to get the feel of it. "Dev-*wuah.* Dev-*wuah.* Dev-*wuah.*" I turned back to my teacher. "*J'ai voudrais—*"

"*Non,*" Suzy said. "Zhee oobli-*yay.*"

"Zhee obli-*yay?*"

"*Ooo,*" she said.

"*Ooo,*" I repeated.

"Zhee ooobli-*yay* dev-*wuah.*"

"Zhee ooobli-*yay* dev-*wuah,*" I repeated. I mouthed the sounds over and over like I had the first time. After several practices, I turned to my teacher. "Zhee ooobli-*yay* dev-*wuah,*" I said with some conviction.

"*Très bien,*" she said. She picked up a piece of paper from her desk and held it out to me.

"*Merci beaucoup,*" I said (all on my own!).

My teacher nodded. I snuck a peek at Suzy, who offered me a sly, conspiratorial smile and a wink.

I left school that day feeling a sense of euphoria. The pronunciation came easily when I simply repeated what Suzy said. I didn't know what the words would look like if they were in front of me, but in that moment, I didn't care. For two seconds after school on a random Tuesday, I'd been fluent in French.

I hit enter a few times and typed up the memory. I titled it *What She Was Like In High School*, which left something to be desired but certainly got to the meat of the matter, and closed the file.

I reached my arms up over my head and stretched. It did wonders to help relieve tension in my shoulders and back. I tipped my head backward and smelled pretzels. This was nuts. Just writing about Suzy led to a scent memory. The mind was a powerful thing.

A man in a black fleece jacket and jeans entered the bullpen. He held a package wrapped in newsprint and tied with twine under his arm. Wendy stood next to him and pointed at me. I turned my head and looked behind me, and, seeing no one, turned back to him. He came toward me. "Samantha Kidd?" he asked.

"Yes. Why?"

"These are for you." He handed me the package. It was soft, and the salty, doughy scent made it clear the imagined pretzel scent was very, very real.

"Someone sent me pretzels?"

"Check your email," he said. He turned and left.

I untied the twine. Under the newsprint was a brown paper bag, and inside the bag were fresh pretzels. And not just any pretzels. Four dozen Philadelphia Soft Pretzels. They were the holy grail of Philadelphia pretzels. Baked fresh daily in a factory in North Philly that was open from six to nine a.m. and only took cash, they were not easy to obtain, but they were worth the effort. And someone who knew how to accrue a debt in his favor had hired a delivery service to bring them to me.

I set the pretzels aside and opened my email. The most recent one was from Joey Carducci, with the subject line "Philadelphia Post Archives."

CHAPTER 16

Sounded Like New Year's Eve

FOUR DOZEN FRESH PRETZELS IS MORE THAN ENOUGH, even for a pretzel connoisseur like me. I separated three pretzels from the bundle and placed them on a napkin next to my monitor, and then called Wendy and asked if she'd set up a station for the staff. Once they were out of my range, I opened Joey's email.

His note was short and sweet, reminding me of our agreement. I saved the attachment. I extracted the files and opened the first one then tore a loop off a pretzel and took a bite before reading. The soft, salty dough tasted better than I remembered. Joey wasn't exactly playing fair; Woodward and Bernstein never bribed each other – or if they did, it wasn't in the movie.

There were multiple articles in the zip file, but the stories of interest were the early ones that reported the facts as the events had unfolded. I'd already heard Suzy's version. Today, I was interested in how the two accounts differed.

According to the *Post*, Suzy Kintz had gone out to dinner with friends the night before Thanksgiving. The dinner took place at a local restaurant known for its intimate setting and extensive wine list, but the group had stuck with the champagne portion of the menu with their meal. One waiter said when he bussed the table, there were more empty bottles than people. "It sounded like New Year's Eve," he said. "They were popping corks every ten minutes."

The dinner lasted for hours, confirmed by both staff and the time stamp on the bill which was charged to Trenton Vega's credit card; he'd made arrangements with the restaurant earlier that day. Suzy was the first to leave sometime after midnight. She called a car service to take her home and left her car parked in the restaurant valet lot.

So far, the story wasn't that different from what Suzy had told me. She'd gone out to dinner with friends. They drank too much, and she called a car to take her home. Her story had been focused on her activities, and the article I now read rounded out the picture with the whereabouts of the others and the confirmation of time from the restaurant. None of those facts were in question. Where was the single piece of damning evidence that made the police sure she'd been the one to commit the crime?

I tore off another piece of pretzel and scanned the rest of the article, and the next, and the next. The fourth page included the narrative report written by the lead detective on the case.

This was what I'd been hoping to find.

The article started with the date. Thanksgiving day, one thirty a.m., seventeen years ago. The detective indicated that dispatch had received a call from the address I now recognized as Suzy's family's compound. Two patrol officers were first to arrive on the scene, and the lead detective and his partner arrived twenty minutes later. He determined that an apparent homicide had occurred inside the bedroom of the guest cottage, secured the perimeter of the property, and contacted the deputy coroner and emergency medical personnel. He further stated that he had positioned another officer at the main entrance of the cottage to maintain the crime scene logbook.

The patrol officers relinquished control of the crime scene to the detective upon arrival, and the detective and his partner signed into the logbook before entering the house. They found Suzy in her terrycloth robe, hair still wet from her shower, sitting in the living room, waiting for their arrival. She led them to the bedroom where her husband lay on the floor. A Sig Sauer P239 handgun lay on the bed. The drawer to the nightstand was open.

The deputy coroner arrived and pronounced Trenton Vega dead at the scene. Trenton's body was transported to the morgue. Suzy was brought in for questioning and detained. It was after midnight, so technically, it was Thanksgiving. The scene was cleared and released twelve hours later.

When a second body, that of a hiker, was discovered eight miles from the Kintz compound, the police looked for a connection. The hiker had been shot with the same caliber handgun as Trenton Vega. It had not mattered that it was the most popular handgun on the market at the time, nor that the gun in question had been found next to Trenton Vega's body, only that the prosecutor could argue a match.

Suzy was tied to that murder as well. Police have

twenty-four hours after detaining someone to get a judge to sign off on a warrant. Weekend days don't count. The holiday weekend worked in law enforcement's favor, and by Monday morning, the arrest warrant was official.

I grabbed a notepad and jotted down questions. *Who else was at dinner? What happened to Suzy's car? Who was the client out with Trenton? What time did Trenton get –*

"Yo, Kidd!"

The sharp call of my name broke my concentration, and I dropped the pen. I looked behind me. Carl was headed my way with a wad of newsprint in his hand. His face was red, and his mouth was turned down. As he got closer, he held the newsprint out. "What did you agree to?"

I shifted my attention from the ball of newsprint to his face and back to the newsprint. He reached my cubicle and threw the crumpled ball onto my notepad. I grabbed the mouse and minimized my computer screen.

"What's that?" he asked. He pointed to the paper.

I flattened it out. It was yesterday's copy of the *Philadelphia Post*. I'd been so excited about the pretzels that Joey had sent that it never occurred to me to cover my tracks. Joey had come through for me, but he'd certainly had some fun in the process.

"Did you get a pretzel?" I asked. "They were delivered fresh from Philadelphia Soft Pretzels. They were still warm when they got here. Wendy put them in the break room."

Carl leaned forward and tapped my spacebar. The computer woke up, and the *Philadelphia Post* article was loud and proud on my screen.

"You gave Joey Carducci your scoop?" he asked. "What kind of a journalist are you? You work here. Your loyalty is to the *Ribbon Eagle*. You should have some loyalty to me, considering I made you a local celebrity and got you this job."

"I can explain," I said.

"Joey Carducci is a tabloid reporter with a petty cash allowance to bribe his sources." He made no secret of his observation of the half pretzel I had left on my napkin (don't judge). "Most people's loyalties aren't so easily bought."

A lot of things have been said about me since I moved back to Ribbon, most of them related to my common sense, and most of them true. But I had two things going for me: I liked to see justice done, and I was loyal to a fault. My closest friends, even Nick, who initially criticized my crime-solving tendencies, came to appreciate what it was like to have me in their corner. Carl could criticize my reporting style, my column's content, or my lack of willpower when faced with fresh pretzels, but I wouldn't let him criticize my loyalty.

I grabbed his wrist and dragged him to the break room. A couple of reporters were at tables. "We need the room," I said. "Everybody out." I jerked my thumb at the door.

Wow. When you give direct instruction, people listen.

When the last of the staff members left the room, I pulled the door shut behind them and flipped the lock. I turned to Carl. "Monty wants me to give him five hundred words on my visit with Suzy by the end of the day. First in a series. All I know is what she told me, and regardless of what I believe, let's just say I recognize she has a very good reason to make herself look innocent. I told you I need to know what the media reported back when it happened. Our archives are light on details, so I made a deal with Joey, and he sent me what they have."

Carl's face turned a heart-attack-indicating shade of red.

"I told him to work with you. Collaborate. Woodward and—"

"Kidd, you talked to Suzy, and you read what Carducci sent over. Do you think there's a story there?"

"*The Post* does," I said. "Isn't that enough to make you curious?"

Carl glared at me. I sensed he had moved past anger to greed. "You owe Carducci nothing. Get back to that prison and get her story. Call me when you're done. This story belongs to us."

CHAPTER 17
Media Wunderkind

I WAS LESS ENTHUSED ABOUT THE ARTICLE I SENT TO my editor than I'd been about pretzel style, but the sheer amount of dough in my system could have been to blame. I had a third cup of coffee after I sent the email, but there's no undoing the lethargy that comes from six soft pretzels in one day. Trust me, I know.

I'd spent the better part of my morning reading articles about Suzy's arrest, and while I was rapidly becoming an expert on her case, I knew next to nothing about her husband, the victim. Investigation can sometimes be as boring as sitting in a chair while searching the internet. You'd think there would be more overweight reporters.

Information about Trenton Vega wasn't hard to find. Of the four pages of hits on Google Search, I started with his obituary. It mentioned his time as CEO of the Vega Group, a media conglomerate that oversaw a family of magazines related to the music industry, and his golden touch when it came to identifying talent and launching acts into the limelight. He and Suzy had been married for three years.

I switched to an image search. Trenton Vega was a good-looking man. He had longish hair that was parted in the middle, sort of Rick Springfield in the "Jesse's Girl" days, and a slight shadow of a beard. His expression was confident. He wore a suit over a shirt with no tie. He held a cigarette in one hand, and a chunky gold wedding band on the same arm as his watch, but no other visible jewelry.

I clicked through the images. It was clear Trenton's lifestyle came with an active social life. There was no shortage of pictures of him surrounded by supermodels and musicians, and despite him being the man behind the media machine, he fit in perfectly. I added Suzy's name to the search field, and the page filled with images of the two of them at parties and events. His arm was always around her waist, and she seemed happy to be with him. If I'd been hoping for daggers in her eyes or jealousy in his expression, I was let down.

Article after article referred to Trenton Vega as a media wunderkind. His father, a publishing mogul, had given him a million dollars when he turned twenty-one and told him to make his fortune. Trenton burned through half of it while partying his way through Europe, eventually befriending the publisher of a group of music magazines. A deal had been struck over a bottle of Chartreuse, and when the men returned stateside, Trenton traded the other half of his inheritance for the acquisition, moved to New York City, and became a magazine magnate like his father.

He sold off a few of the publications he acquired and consolidated the rest. He rebranded and bankrolled the first few issues himself, which gave him the freedom to write what he wanted to write without answering to advertising pressure. He included endorsements for products he believed in, and when he sent copies of the publication to the companies he endorsed, they responded favorably with advertising dollars of their own. Soon, the magazine paid for itself, and he started a division of the Vega Group for talent management and promotion. He'd been on Forbes's "Thirty under Thirty" list and Fortune's "Forty under Forty." He'd been forty-nine when he died.

The circumstances surrounding his murder gave the Vega Group even more attention, and a management group continued the business. At last valuation, it was priced at fifty million dollars.

Fifty million dollars.

My recent windfall had changed my monetary picture overnight, but my financial manager liked to remind me that I was far from independently wealthy. Fifty million was independently wealthy. But with Trenton Vega being dead, who benefited?

People who don't have money think the best thing about having money is, well, having money. And they're mostly right. But there's a great side benefit, which is having a financial officer who takes your calls. Ellison Wirth was mine.

The receptionist put me through right away (I told her I had a time-sensitive investment opportunity to discuss), and Ellison picked up. "Samantha, nice to hear from you. We're not scheduled to review your portfolio until next month."

"I know, but this can't wait. Would you say a media company is a good investment?"

The nice thing about finance guys, I've found, is they don't pass judgment on ideas that come out of the blue.

Where other people saw the world in black and white, Ellison saw it in green. If I wanted to invest in a project, he was a reliable source of intel for the risk assessment.

"Media is a gamble if you don't have the right contacts. Start-up costs are high, and you'll need to quickly get your finger on the pulse of the industry. It's a safer bet to put your money into property management."

"What about buying a magazine that's already established?"

"Unless you know something about the industry, you're going to put a lot of money into something with no promise of a return while carrying a heavy debt load. Media companies tend to underperform during times of economic stress and overdeliver during upswings. I can look at your portfolio and diversify into media if you want, but most clients who want a piece of the media pie either think it's sexy or have ties to the business. It's not a strategy I recommend."

I was confused. Everything I'd just read about Trenton Vega suggested he took a moderate investment and parlayed it into a fifty-million-dollar enterprise, but Ellison made it sound like media companies were the shiny red sportscar of an investor's portfolio.

"If it's a risky proposition, then why do people buy them?"

"Power, mostly. Earnings come from advertising, but ownership provides a platform for news, propaganda, promotion, and trend forecasting. Insiders like the investment so they can influence public opinion."

Ellison was born to be a financial planner, and part of his responsibility was to inform me about strategy but let me make the decisions. I was so used to the people in my life wanting to know *why* I thought what I thought and did what I did that talking to someone who answered my questions without commentary was new. I loved having a financial planner!

But aside from the mention of trend forecasting (which would allow me to endorse Nick's new venture and give him a leg up in the sneaker world) I had no interest in owning a media company, and the general information I'd gained from Ellison hadn't moved the needle on my investigation. Before he started talking about EBITDA and bear markets, I changed course.

"I read about a media company that was started for five hundred thousand dollars and recently was valued at fifty million. Why can't I do that?" Silence. "Ellison? Are you still there?"

Ellison coughed. He cleared his throat a few times and then spoke. "Samantha, last month you wanted to buy an abandoned shopping mall and turn it into an apartment complex. Two months ago, you wanted to open a chain of coffee shops that roasted their beans in pizza ovens. Your husband is launching a sneaker business, and I've already told you that's your best bet in terms of acquisitions."

"And I've told you he won't take my money."

Ellison sighed. "It's not that I don't appreciate your interest in diversifying your portfolio, but as I've explained each time, there are variables we look at, and with clients your age, we recommend a steady investment plan that will yield a tidy sum when you retire. Get-rich-quick opportunities only work for investors who are already rich."

"But it worked for the Vega Group," I said. "Trenton Vega couldn't have just gotten lucky."

"Oh. Yes. That story has been in the news lately. Samantha, I think it's best to follow the strategy we laid out for you. I'll keep my ears open for investment opportunities that align with your interests, but I should caution you that the meteoric growth factor of the Vega Group was an anomaly. That company was on the verge of bankruptcy when he died."

"How is that possible?"

"Simple. The publicity surrounding his murder brought a lot of attention to his media holdings. Trenton Vega was in financial straits when he died, but his murder made his investors very rich men."

CHAPTER 18

No Stranger to Scandal

"WHAT HAPPENED TO THE VEGA GROUP? IS HIS BOARD still running it?" I asked.

"No." Ellison spoke confidently about the details as if he'd read them this morning. "Trenton's father had controlling interest in the Vega Group, and after the fifty-million valuation, he sold it to a media conglomerate."

"When was this?"

"Shortly after his son's murder. Different times," he said.

I thanked Ellison for his time and hung up. I'd gotten sound investment advice, and a new motive. It seemed unlikely that a group of investors had hired a hitman to take out Trenton Vega, but fifty million was too much money to ignore. And was it curious that just yesterday I'd seen Conrad Vega at Loncar's office, wanting to hire a detective? I didn't know what to make of that just yet.

It wasn't the first time someone had mentioned the financial implications of Trenton Vega's murder. Monty had said that scandal sells papers. And what had Carl told me?

Scandal is good for business. And now Ellison, with the mention of free publicity.

Ellison had also mentioned Nick's business. Which might be why my mind strayed from Suzy Kintz's husband to mine. Nick needed name recognition, and the answer was right in front of me: Nick needed a scandal.

I was no stranger to scandal. In fact, the article Carl had written about me started as a profile and ended with the scandal that left me with a chunk of money in the bank and Eddie out of work. It was also the last time I'd tried to help Nick with his business, and it hadn't gone as swimmingly as I would have liked, so whatever scandal I came up with was going to have to happen without his knowledge. It was going to be hard to scandalize Nick in public and not damage his reputation.

It was going to have to happen in private. And it was going to have to make Nick look like a rock star. And it was going to have to seem like something he would never do on his own. I remembered something Geri Loncar had said when she mentioned Suzy Kintz and I got an idea.

Fortunately, Nick viewed my impulse to help people as charming, because my idea was going to require his participation as well. I was going to make Nick's sneaker company a household name by leaking a sex tape.

Two DAYS PASSED before my next visit with Suzy. Two days to consider the flaws in my plan. Two days where I conducted research. Two days to scope out the perfect location for a camera that would maintain a respectable distance from the bed.

There is a surprising amount of information online when it comes to making a naughty at home video (and, curiously, a lot of advice not to do it. But they didn't understand that I had good intentions. I'm sure if I could explain myself, they'd feel differently.) I read articles on *Maxim, Cosmo, Women's Health*, and *WikiHow*. It was like the time I researched how to make the best grilled cheese sandwich.

I ordered a Diva Light Ring and tripod and watched a Masterclass on filmmaking. To keep Nick from getting suspicious, I kept my notes in a most-non-sexy pink file folder with a picture of a kitten on the front. I also cleaned the house, organized his sock drawer, and learned how to make a pie crust from scratch. I let the laundry pile build up, though; too much domesticity would definitely let him know something was up! Forty-eight hours later, I was convinced my plan would work.

My plan for Nick kept me distracted from the news and the gossip surrounding Suzy. I wanted to know her side of things without preamble, and the only way to do so was to avoid the media.

The morning of the second visit, I dressed in a dove-gray pullover and matching trousers paired with low-heeled black Chelsea boots with a kitten heel. I was more excited than I'd been the first time; today, I had an agenda.

Nick and I walked out together even though we were headed different directions. The SUV was parked in the driveway next to Nick's white pickup truck.

"You've been watching the news, right?" I asked him. "Do you think she did it?"

"Kidd, I thought the reason you were avoiding the latest rehash of her case was so you could form your own opinion."

"Yes, but I'd like to hear what you think."

"This is your thing," he said. "Until I come up with a profit and media strategy for my sneaker launch, I can't think of much else."

Inside, I beamed. I had Nick's problem all worked out! (Or I would after I picked up a burner phone for filming. You didn't think I was going to use my personal phone and accidentally upload our video to the cloud, did you?)

I circled the SUV to unplug the cord from the exterior electrical outlet, but the cord was already disconnected. "Did you disconnect my car from the outlet?" I asked.

Nick stooped down. "Maybe you didn't have it plugged in all the way, and it fell out."

"Maybe," I said. I remembered Kent from Tanner Auto telling me that the SUV hadn't been fully charged, but I didn't want to believe this had been my fault. Maybe someone wanted me to be stuck at home. Maybe someone who had recently learned that I'd developed an interest in electric cars. Maybe a certain cop-turned-private-investigator had snuck by the house and unplugged the loaner to keep me detained. I didn't float this theory to Nick because some things sound a little paranoid when said out loud.

"Is there any chance you can give me a ride?" I asked.

He shook his head. "I've got back-to-back Zoom meetings with possible spokespeople starting in an hour. There's no way I can make it back in time to be prepared. If you plug it in now, maybe you'll have enough juice to get to Tanner Auto."

"Maybe," I said again. I plugged the car in and kissed Nick goodbye, waited for him to leave, and then pulled the cord out. If someone had done this to keep me stranded, I certainly wasn't going to let them know their plan hadn't worked.

I went back inside and called Eddie. "Yo," I said. "I need a favor."

"What else is new?"

I begged for a ride, and he relented. And while I waited for him to arrive, I added him to my list of problems to solve.

———

I DIRECTED Eddie to the designated visitor parking on the lower level. With no press conference scheduled, the lots were empty save for a scattering of cars that belonged to the employees. I agreed to call him when I was out, and he agreed to wait. The last thing I heard were the sounds of Candy Crush Saga coming from his phone.

I signed in, put my belongings in a locker, and submitted to the pat-down. I followed the prison guard to the visitor room. This time other prisoners and guests were in there too. A few people glanced at me, but none seemed particularly interested in my arrival. I bought two cups of coffee and carried them to an empty round table, where I sat and waited. A few minutes later, the doors opened, and Suzy walked in.

The last time I was here, I'd been struck by how little she'd changed since high school. Today, I found myself wondering how that could be. Her hair was glossy and brown. Her lips were stained red. Her skin was blemish-free. These weren't hallmarks of a lifer.

"I wasn't sure you'd come back," she said.

"I have questions."

"I'm sure you do." She lowered herself into the chair opposite me. I pushed my spare coffee cup toward her, and she pulled off the lid and inhaled the scent. "Fire away," she said.

"How do you keep your hair looking so healthy?"

"Coffee grinds and olive oil." She sipped the hot coffee.

"Is it easy to get olive oil in prison?"

"No," she said. "It's not."

Suzy leaned against the back of her chair. In a completely unplanned way, our outfits were coordinated. Today Suzy wore a dark-gray sweatshirt and light-gray sweatpants. The collar of the sweatshirt was shredded from too many washings, though the last time I went shopping, I'd seen similar deconstructed styles for sale with a three-digit price tag. White socks and sneakers. The other prisoners wore similar outfits in a lighter shade of gray. Once again, Suzy had found a way to look different from everybody else.

"Why are your sweats darker gray than everybody else's?"

A smile played at the corners of her mouth. "I work laundry detail. When something interesting shows up, I get first pick."

"That doesn't put you at odds with your, um, roommates?"

"I worked that out a long time ago."

"Did you really film a sex tape?"

She tipped her head and smiled, though it appeared as though the smile were more for her than me. "You threw me off with that one."

"Did you?"

"It was a private video that became public when Trenton decided he needed some free publicity. We filmed it while in Saint-Jean-Cap-Ferrat on our honeymoon." Geri had heard right. It sounded classy. "If I claimed self-defense and that tape was admitted into evidence, nobody would have believed I didn't love my husband." She toyed with her coffee cup. "These aren't the questions I expected you to ask."

I hadn't worked out the best way to get Suzy to talk, and now that she was in front of me talking, I was at a loss. While time may have been the one commodity she had in droves, my clock was ticking. I chose the direct approach.

"What happened that night?"

At this, she seemed surprised. "You don't know? It's all over the news. I took three back-to-back laundry shifts just to avoid the gossip."

"I'm good at sticking my head in the sand when properly motivated."

"What about when it happened?"

"I lived in New York at the time and had my own concerns."

"Then what do you know?"

"A little. Not enough." I leaned forward. "Conrad Vega hired a local private investigator. I'd hoped to talk to the investigator about you, but it's probably fair to say he won't see things your way."

"Is he any good?"

"Retired homicide detective. He taught me everything I know."

"Is that supposed to make me feel better?"

I considered every time Loncar had told me to do one thing and I'd done the other. "Probably not."

A heavyset woman in snug sweats walked past our table. She looked directly at me and held my stare for a moment, then at Suzy. The two of them nodded at each other.

"Some of these women are here for a few years. Drugs, possession, aggravated assault. I've watched them come and go. Most of them steer clear of me. Thanks to the media, my story is public knowledge. When women hear they're coming to this facility, they make up their minds about me before we've ever met."

"You've never wanted to tell your side of things? Just once? You didn't even take the stand at your trial."

"I thought you didn't know anything about my case."

"There was a reporter from Philly here the day of the press conference. I read his story. He's doing a series."

"Yes, stories about rich people falling from grace sell a lot of papers."

"I'm here now, and my ride doesn't expect me back out there for at least an hour. You said if I came back, you'd answer any questions I had about that night."

Her brow furrowed. She took a cigarette out of the pack on the table and flipped it so the filter was pointing down and then tapped it on the surface of the table. "Your ride?"

"I had car trouble this morning."

"Anything serious?"

"These days, I'm sort of vehicle-challenged. Nothing long-term."

Suzy was less relaxed today than on my first visit. I hadn't noticed it at first, but something had changed. It was as if she'd been expecting something from me and I hadn't produced. One of my driving forces in life was anticipating what people wanted and overdelivering, so the sense that I'd let her down was hard to ignore.

I leaned forward. "This can't just be about the prisoner confession and your chance at a new trial. There's something you're not telling me. You keep saying you want me to find out about your case on my time, but if you want so badly to get out of here, then you're going to have to tell me something."

Suzy glanced over both shoulders. For the first time since I'd met her in high school, she seemed concerned by what other people might think. "You said your ride expected you in an hour. This might take a little longer than that."

CHAPTER 19

Crazy Fast Courtship

"BUY ME A FRESH CUP OF COFFEE?" SUZY SAID.

"Sure." I left her at the table and quickly returned with two new (overpriced) cups of steaming black swill. (The prison commissary made Starbucks look like charity.) I set one in front of her and kept the other for myself. One sip indicated I was about to get my caffeine allotment for the week.

"I married Trenton Vega when I was nineteen," Suzy said after sipping her beverage. "He was forty-six. His dad owned a media empire, and I did some freelance styling. We met at a party in Milan and were inseparable for two weeks. Even though there were over two decades between our ages, he understood me. My life. He felt like an equal, and that was something I'd never known before."

"How long did that last?"

She grew wistful. "We got married before we left Europe and the honeymoon lasted almost six months." She toyed with the cigarette in front of her, flipping it over and over between her hands. "I started to believe it was real."

"What happened?"

"We came back and Trenton started the Vega Group. I quickly discovered he wasn't a nice man. He supplied drugs to clients and made backroom deals. He cheated on me constantly. Once he locked me in a closet for three days and let one of his bands use the apartment for . . . stuff."

My stomach turned. This was background information, the sort of thing that might have painted a different picture of Suzy if she'd testified. But she had remained silent through the arrest, the trial, and the reading of the verdict. Even in high school, she'd been detached from her surroundings. I remembered what Eddie said about her paintings, about that corner of the canvas she'd left empty.

"Why did you stay with him?"

She toyed with the coffee cup in front of her. "You don't just get up and leave a man like Trenton Vega without a plan." She took another drink, this one longer.

"Did you tell anybody this stuff? Either before or after the murder?"

She studied me for a second. "Do you know what the psychiatrist said at my trial?"

"No."

"Someone who kills a loved one for purely selfish reasons might hold on to the sense that they're a victim because they don't want to process what they did. They're completely aware of the crime they committed, but they maintain the sense that they've been vindicated."

"Was this psychiatrist arguing for you or against you?"

"Hard to tell, isn't it?" She pulled a fresh cigarette from the pack and held it up to her lips. "Trenton Vega was shot with a Sig Sauer P239 handgun. Did you know that?"

"Yes," I said. "I read the police transcripts. Is that significant?"

"He told me he was worried about a new client. He wanted a gun for self-defense. My family always had guns around, so I told him I'd find him something suitable. Guess what I bought him?"

"A Sig Sauer P239?"

She nodded. "None of this is familiar?"

"I told you, I wasn't around when it happened. When I left Ribbon, I didn't look back. I lost ties with everybody from high school."

"How about now? How long have you been back?"

"It's been a few years."

"And?"

And aside from Eddie, who I'd reconnected with by accident, I hadn't gone out of my way to meet up with the old crowd. Most of my close circle of high school friends had scattered out into the country like I had, and after the initial flurry of letters and phone calls, we established our lives, the futures we'd each wanted for ourselves, and lost touch.

Social media had made it easy to post throwback photos and tag old friends, but the more I saw the lives those friends now lived, the more I wondered if it were better to leave those memories as they were and not stare into the chasm of our modern-day differences. Moving back had given me an opportunity to reassess who I was and where I was headed, but the simple life I thought I wanted was an illusion. I'd run toward chaos so many times since coming back to Ribbon that it was ignorant to pretend I didn't like it.

"What was high school like for you?" I asked.

"Weren't you there?"

"I don't think we went to the same high school." I paused.

"You might be right."

She leaned back, lit a match, and held the flame close to the end of her cigarette. She inhaled, just like she had the first day I visited, closed her eyes, and then exhaled. Two streams of smoke came out of her nostrils. She opened her eyes and stared at the cigarette between her fingers. Slowly, she lowered the cigarette to the ashtray and stamped it out.

"I was expelled from three different prep schools before I ended up at Ribbon High. My parents gave me an ultimatum. I had to get a high school degree to get my trust fund. By the time I was sixteen, they didn't care where that degree came from. Dawn wanted to work in the family business, but I wanted to see the world."

"Is Dawn your sister?"

"Yes," she paused. "I drove to the airport after graduation and bought a one-way ticket to Europe. Bummed around for a bit, met some interesting people, had some fun. When I met Trenton, everything changed."

A feeling of unease settled over me while Suzy talked. She was likeable, but it felt too much like her narrative had been crafted over time, whittled into a bow designed to play against my heartstrings. She'd told me to find out about her case before returning, but now, confronted with the breadcrumbs she sprinkled at my feet, it seemed impossible that she'd been convicted of murder.

"Do you like pretzels?" she asked.

"Is the Pope Catholic?" I answered. She smiled. "I'm

probably among the top one percent of pretzel connoisseurs."

"You spend your formative years in a pretzel factory, and you have no idea what the world is like. It seems so simple."

"It couldn't have been all bad."

"Remember what I said about your appetite?" she asked.

I nodded.

"That's what I meant. A healthy appetite for food usually indicates a healthy appetite for life. I was right about that, wasn't I? You left Ribbon and tasted life."

"Yes, but I came back."

"Yes. But coming back after you left isn't the same as not leaving. What you get from this town now is a new experience too. You're no more the same person from Ribbon High than I am." She shook a second cigarette from the pack but didn't light it. "You start to think this can't be all there is, and then you go out to learn for yourself. And you end up in a cage." She shook her head as if trying to shake off the memories. "I used to say the pretzel factory was a prison. If only I'd known then what I know now."

I couldn't justify the rich girl who'd appeared to have everything with the woman in front of me, and I couldn't understand how we'd both attended the same high school but had become such wildly different people.

"I lost my virginity in the factory," she said wistfully. "To this day, the smell of fresh pretzels reminds me of sex."

Maybe we weren't so different after all?

The door behind Suzy opened, and the prison guard who'd patted me down came in. "Kintz!" she yelled.

Suzy turned slowly and looked at her.

"Visit's over."

"I thought visiting hours were until eight p.m.?" I asked.

The guard gestured for me to stand. "Visits are a privilege and can be revoked at any time. You violated the terms of your stay."

I looked from Suzy's somewhat surprised face to the guard's and back to Suzy's. "What did I do?"

Suzy shrugged.

"What did I do?" I asked the guard.

"No loitering on the property or in the parking lot."

"How can I be loitering if I'm in here?"

"There's a man in a Volkswagen Bug who claims to be your ride. He's been wandering the perimeter of the building unsupervised for the past hour. That's loitering."

Eddie.

"He's my ride," I said.

"Against the rules. Let's go."

I put my hands on the table and pushed my chair back. Suzy grabbed my wrist and kept me from standing. "My things were moved to a storage locker on the outskirts of town. Go see my parents at the pretzel store and tell them you need the key. Use whatever you want. And Samantha? Next time you come back, come back alone."

CHAPTER 20

A Preapproved Walk on the Wild Side

THE PRISON GUARD MOVED CLOSER TO OUR TABLE, AND Suzy released her grip on my wrist. I stood. I couldn't look away from her face. Without moving her head, her eyes shifted to the right. The prison guard was next to her, facing me. Suzy's eyes shifted back to mine, and they were damp with unshed tears. She mouthed, "Please."

"Let's go," the guard said.

I stepped away from the table and followed the guard. I didn't look back. The silence that fell over the room felt prickly. If Suzy had spent the past seventeen years playing the lifer who was untouchable, then she'd risked it all when she let her emotions show. I still didn't know if it was an act. And whatever happened, I needed to at least know that.

I collected my things and left. Eddie's VW was idling by the curb. I hopped in and buckled up, and he took off. We didn't speak until we were half a mile away.

"Dude! You are not going to believe what happened," he said.

"You got tired of sitting in your car, so you got out to

stretch your legs. And then you thought it would be fun to see the prison, and you walked out of the lower parking lot to the sidewalk. Some prison guards came over to talk to you, and the next thing you know, you were told to get your car because my visit was over."

Eddie shot me a look of incredulity. "How'd you know?"

"You violated the terms of my visitation rights," I said. I stared out the window while we drove past a farmhouse sitting isolated in the middle of several acres of property. "I don't know if they're going to let me come back."

"You're enjoying this, aren't you? It's a preapproved walk on the wild side with the popular girl."

"It's nothing like that," I said. I kept staring out the window, this time past a hillside of cattle grazing. "Do you think that's why I'm doing this?"

"No judgment," he said. "But I know you. There's no way going into that prison didn't get your pulse pounding."

"Yes, but there's something else. This is a person who once looked like she had everything and now she has nothing, and for seventeen years she's been okay with that."

"But not anymore."

"Right." Normally, I liked to chat things through with either Eddie or Nick, but today, I was pensive. I couldn't define what it was that captivated me about Suzy in the past and now. All I knew was that I had to know more. "What's on your schedule for today?"

"Canvassing the area for jobs, mostly. Do you want me to take you home?"

"Yes," I said slowly. "But let's stop at Kintz Pretzels on the way."

———

For as busy as the soft pretzel store had been earlier, the parking lot to Kintz Pretzels was empty. Two cars were parked in the back by the factory, and a flush crept over my cheeks as I remembered what Suzy had said. I wondered, briefly, if there was a way to sneak inside after hours and film my risqué video with Nick but dismissed the thought quickly. There was no way I could maintain my focus on Nick while inside the factory where the pretzel magic happened.

Eddie followed me inside and wandered around the product displays while I waited by the register for an employee to greet me.

A skinny teenaged girl with a long brown ponytail came out from the back. "Can I help you?" she asked.

"Maybe. Is there a manager here?"

"Tom and Katy are here. Do you want to talk to one of them?"

That wasn't a no. "Sure."

"Which one?"

I shrugged. "Either," I said. "Or both."

"Hold on." She left me by the counter and disappeared into the back.

Eddie approached the counter with four bags of unsalted artisan pretzels. "These people have no idea how to merchandise their showroom. It's a travesty." He set the bags down. "Aren't you getting anything?"

"I'm in the middle of something," I hissed under my breath.

The teen reappeared between the swinging doors to the

factory with a stout, past-middle-aged couple. The man wore a white shirt and black pants that were being held up with suspenders. The woman was frail. She wore a peach sweatshirt, khaki pants, and Crocs. The trio paused while the doors were open, finishing up a conversation out of earshot.

"Holy cow, those are the Kintzes," Eddie said.

I turned to him. "The owners?"

"Yep. They did an event at Tradava about ten years ago. Before you moved back to Ribbon. The department managers were at an off-site meeting to get inspired, and the store manager lined up a day of guest speakers from local businesses. Tom got the spot after lunch, and between the hoagies and the pretzels, people dozed off. The store manager was mortified."

This was fortuitous. I straightened to my full height and smiled. I didn't look at Eddie. "Give me five minutes, okay?" I said out of the side of my mouth.

He tapped the bags of pretzels he'd set on the counter. "Fine, but I'm not leaving without these."

Eddie disappeared behind a row of boxes that had been cut open and stacked so customers could help themselves to bags of pretzels. I shifted my position so the pretzel wall was fully behind me.

"The young lady said you wanted to talk to us?" Tom Kintz said.

I had to contain my enthusiasm. Meeting the owner of a six-generation pretzel company was a little like meeting Elvis. "Hi," I said. "I'm Samantha Kidd. I work for the *Ribbon Eagle*."

They turned toward each other, and a world of communication was shared in that glance. Katy turned her back on me, and Tom's face got dark. "We have no comment for the press."

"No! That's not why I'm here," I said quickly. "I went to school with Suzy," I added, and then, because the cooped-up adrenaline over meeting pretzel royalty now spilled out into verbal diarrhea, continued. "I just came from the prison. I met with her. I went to help her. She told me to come see you." My words fell on their turned backs.

Tom had his hand on the swinging door, and Katy was only marginally behind him, but something I said seemed to stop her forward momentum. She turned back around.

"You saw our Suzy?"

"Yes."

"She approved your request to visit?"

"It was her idea. She made the arrangements through her lawyer, and he contacted me."

Tom and Katy looked at each other again, and this time, whatever unspoken words were shared, they were softer. And just as I thought I'd won their trust, a loud explosion from the pretzel factory behind them claimed whatever attention I'd gained.

CHAPTER 21

All the Advertising Money in the World Can't Overcome That

Tom Kintz turned and ran through the swinging doors, faster than I would have imagined a man his weight moving. Katy seemed torn between following him and staying with me. I felt her conflict.

"I need to know what happened that night," I said. "Suzy told me to come see you to get a key to her storage locker."

"I don't know anything about a storage locker," Katy said. "I'm sorry." She turned and left, following her husband. I felt my shoulders slump and the smile drop from my face. This was another dead end.

The doors swung open, and a younger, female version of Tom Kintz appeared. The woman had the same stout build, same dark coloring, same turned-up nose and dimples.

"There was a man here earlier asking questions about Suzy," she said. "He said he was hired to investigate the case for an independent party. Are you working for him?"

"I work for the *Ribbon Eagle*, but I'm here because Suzy

told me to come." I smiled. "You're Dawn, aren't you?" I asked. "Suzy's sister."

Pink spots colored the woman's cheeks, and she looked away from me. "Suzy got the glamour. I'm a people person." She looked back and smiled, and her dimples deepened. I could see how she'd make a great representative of the company; her cherub-like face and sweet demeanor would charm the hardest heart.

"This man who came here today – did he look like a police detective trying to pass himself off as a regular guy?" I asked.

Dawn nodded. She opened a drawer below the cash register and pulled out a white business card. She held it out so I could read it. The words "Loncar Investigations" were printed on the front above a phone number and address. "We run a business, and part of that means we don't talk about what happened. Not to the press, and not to strangers who say they're representing an independent party."

"He's working for Conrad Vega," I said. "I don't know who else he's talked to, but he's persistent. He'll probably come back."

She stared at Loncar's business card and then dropped it back into the drawer. She pulled out a maple wood keychain carved into the letters "S.K." "After Suzy was arrested, my parents sealed up the guest cottage. When the lawyer sent over his files, I put them out there too." She held out the keychain. "Maybe you'll find something that can help."

I closed my fingers around the keyring, and as I took possession, I felt the weight of Dawn Kintz's expectations settle onto my shoulders.

The doors to the factory swung open again, and Tom appeared. "Dawn, the main pretzel oven blew a fuse. We're going to have to shut down production today."

"I'll call maintenance," she said to him. She wrote an address on the back of Loncar's business card and handed it to me.

As she followed her dad into the back, Eddie appeared at my side. "Did you hear that?" he asked. "They're closing down production for the day. I wonder what happens to the pretzels that were par-baked? Knowing you, you didn't hear anything that woman said because you're busy imagining how pretzels taste hot off the conveyor belt."

Funny thing: the thought hadn't even crossed my mind.

———

WE DIDN'T STICK AROUND to find out what goes into the fixing of a broken pretzel oven. I jammed the key and card into my handbag and followed Eddie to his car. It was well after lunch, and my debt to Eddie had snowballed beyond our usual dynamic. He was in oddly good spirits despite the lack of caffeine in the previous four hours and agreed to my offer to buy him a hoagie without protest.

B&S Sandwiches had four locations around town, and I placed our order at the one I'd patronized the least. It wasn't a systematic attempt to try them all that informed my decision, but rather, location; my GPS indicated that B&S Sandwich location #4 was nearest the Kintz residence to which I now had a key.

We ordered two large hoagies on hard rolls, Eddies with

vinegar, mine without. He claimed a table while I snagged a large bag of chips and two bottles of Icy Tea and paid. The sandwiches were ready shortly thereafter, and I carried the pair of lunch meat torpedoes to where he sat.

Eddie unwrapped his sandwich and immediately removed half of the meat. He reassembled the rest and bit. "Do you think a company like that knows what they have?" Eddie asked after he swallowed.

"You mean Kintz Pretzels? How could they not?"

"You're a pretzel connoisseur, and you don't buy Kintz pretzels. How come?"

I neatly stacked five slices of tomato on my wax paper and tried to close my sandwich. It was still too big to fit in my mouth. I opened it again and took off the cappicola and then squeezed the roll shut and tried again. The hard roll had softened thanks to the drizzle of oil, but it still took a little work to eat it. This was the beauty of a hoagie. It required just enough effort to eat that you felt like you'd somehow earned the stupor that inevitably settled in when you were done.

After I swallowed, I ran my tongue over my teeth and set the half sandwich down. "We never had Kintz pretzels around when I was a kid. We had Snyder's, Splitz, and Sturgis. When we wanted soft pretzels, we went to Philly Pretzel Factory."

"Yes, but you don't do things because you did them growing up. I've seen how you think. You're curious. You have to have more of a reason not to eat Kintz pretzels than that."

I took another bite and chewed. There was another reason, and it had nothing to do with the quality, price, availability, or familiarity of the brand. It had to do with petty teenaged jealousy.

"Remember how people treated Suzy when she first showed up in high school?"

"I wasn't there, remember? I transferred in senior year. She was a stranger just like everybody else. Why? Did she get hazed or something?"

"She wanted nothing to do with anybody. She had her own car in tenth grade."

"That's right. The white Audi convertible. Sweet car." He picked up the open bag of chips and dumped a pile on his wax paper.

"She used to leave during lunch. Just get in her car and drive away, and nobody knew where she went. So naturally, the rumors started."

"Were they nice?"

"It was tenth grade, and she was the rich new girl. What do you think?" I asked.

He nodded his head as if he saw my point.

"Half of the school wanted to hate her because she was rich, and half of the school wanted to be her best friend —"

"— because she was rich."

"Right."

"Which side were you on?"

"Neither," I said immediately, and then added, "Both." I was quiet for a moment. "We were always friendly but never became friends. I didn't gossip about her because that seemed petty, but I didn't fawn all over her either. I think I was jealous of what she had on the surface, the money, the car, the freedom, the pretzels, but on some level, I saw how isolated she was, and I knew she wasn't happy. I think I equated sadness with Kintz pretzels."

"All the advertising money in the world can't overcome that."

We finished our hoagies (at least the better part of them), bussed our table, and left. Up to this point, I'd kept quiet about the keys Suzy's sister handed me when we left the pretzel store, but the desire to hold on to the attention Suzy had given me when she arranged for me to visit was eerily similar to the attention I felt when she was nice to me in high school. I needed a neutral party to help me see things objectively, and sitting to my left was one I'd just filled with cured meats and fried potatoes. I figured that had accrued me some good will.

I pulled the keychain out of my handbag and dangled it between us. "Dawn Kintz gave me this. It holds the answers to every question we have about Suzy. I know I owe you more than a sandwich for being my chauffeur. Any chance your schedule is open this afternoon?"

———

THE KINTZ FAMILY compound was about a mile east of the sandwich shop. Eddie followed the directions given by Siri, which could have been simplified to "the million-dollar mansion in the middle of farmland."

Calling the house behind the house a guest cottage was modest at best. It was a three-story structure with a two-car garage. It had a separate address on a property that could have accommodated the von Trapps with square footage to spare. Eddie turned on a private road that led to the entrance and parked outside the garage doors.

We sat in the car and stared at the building. Neither one of us rushed to get out. Dawn Kintz had said that the files on Suzy's case were inside, but there was something else about it that I couldn't deny. Something familiar. I opened my handbag and pulled out the folded-up front page of the *Philadelphia Post* I'd been carrying around since our breakfast days ago and flattened it in my lap. The picture that accompanied the photo was a three-story house surrounded by cornfields. I held the paper up so Eddie could see what I saw: the building to which I now held the keys was the site of the murder.

Interesting that Dawn Kintz hadn't thought to mention that.

CHAPTER 22
A Solution to One Problem

"Is that where . . .?" Eddie asked.

"I think so."

"Has anybody. . . ?"

"I don't know."

"Are you still. . . ?"

"Yes."

Eddie and I had developed a verbal shorthand and often communicated without full sentences. It was convenient both in saving time and making sure we weren't being eavesdropped upon. Occasionally it led to a gross misunderstanding, but since misunderstandings between us usually had to do with food, the outcome was usually a win-win.

I tucked the paper away and got out of Eddie's VW Bug. He didn't move. I was going in, but knowing what I now knew, I'd leave it up to him to decide if he wanted to follow me.

It took a little effort to fit the key into the lock and a little more to jiggle it open. Pine needles and cobwebs had jammed the hinges, but eventually, my efforts were rewarded. The door swung inward, and I entered. I turned and looked at the VW.

Eddie got out and slammed his door. "I don't know why I let you drag me into these things."

"You can wait in the car if you want," I said.

"And miss seeing how a pretzel heiress and her media mogul husband rolled while in Ribbon? No way."

By the time I crossed the threshold, Eddie was right behind me. The interior of the house was dank. A beam of light pierced a gap between the curtains, and the minimal movement of opening the front door stirred up dust particles that now floated through the air. I flipped the lights switch to the On position, but nothing happened. After several more on/off flips, I abandoned the light switch and went deeper inside in the dark. Eddie used the flashlight app on his phone behind me.

White sheets had been thrown over the furniture in the living room. I peeked under and saw a tufted mahogany-brown leather sofa. The hide was buttery soft to the touch. Another sheet revealed a coffee table, and sheets across from the sofa revealed two museum-quality antique nutwood chairs upholstered in green velvet. Even without an appraiser, I knew the furniture was expensive.

I followed Eddie through the living room to the dining room. Cardboard cartons were stacked alongside a wall, each marked with a range of dates and notations pertaining to Suzy's case. I lifted the lid from the box on the end and pulled out a yellowed newspaper. It was the issue that ran the first details about the murder. I dug through the stack of newspapers in the carton. This was what I needed. Not just the facts, but the public opinion as well. It was no different than high school. What people said about Suzy was simply a reflection of how they felt about themselves: were they jealous? Envious? Or craving attention?

"Dude," Eddie said. I looked up. He stood in the doorway with his phone in his hand. "I just got a text from my Christmas ornament supplier. He's got two hundred vintage Soviet pinecone ornaments that I can have for pennies on the dollar if I come get them right now."

"It's March."

"Vintage soviet ornaments don't turn up every day, and if I don't take them, they'll get dumped in a landfill or snatched by an Etsy crafter."

I pointed to the boxes. "I need to go through these."

"It's too dark to see anything. You need to come back with a couple of thousand-candle-watt flashlights."

"I don't want to wait. By the time I get home and come back with the SUV, it'll be dark. And creepy. And, I don't know, I just feel like the clock is ticking."

"Are you allowed to take stuff from the house?"

"Suzy said I could take what I wanted from her storage locker, but her family didn't know anything about that. This is the same thing, right? What did you find?"

"Something that might solve one of your problems." He held up a set of keys dangling from an Audi key fob.

"Are those the keys to Suzy's Cabriolet?"

He nodded.

"Did you see it?"

"There's a garage."

In the fading light of the day, I led Eddie out the back door, across the lawn, to the two-car garage. Despite the wealth of the Kintz family, they hadn't invested in high-tech gadgets to modernize their farm. There was a touch pad for keyless entry mounted to the right of the garage door, but without the code, it seemed foolish to make random guesses and potentially set off an alarm. I stepped back and searched for a keyhole, and when I located it, stooped and tried various keys. The third one worked. I rolled the garage door up and stared at the same white Audi Cabriolet that Suzy had driven in high school.

The car was cleaner than it should have been considering the owner had been unavoidably detained. I ran my hand over the curve of the hood and trailed my fingers across the door. I tried the remote, but nothing happened. The key fob was a few decades old, but it worked similarly to my late, lamented Honda del Sol. I opened the fob to reveal the key and then inserted it in the door and turned. The locks fell open. I pulled on the door handle and slipped onto the black leather seat.

"Do we think this is okay?" I asked Eddie. "I don't want to get arrested for grand theft auto."

"Then I'll take you home after I pick up the ornaments. It was just a thought."

I ran my hands over the wheel and the dashboard. The interior was pristine. This wasn't a car that had been sitting ignored. Someone, probably a family member, had cared for it in her absence. I unlocked the glove box and found the registration, current, in Suzy's name. I moved the key to the ignition and tried to start the car. The engine responded with a cough and a sputter, but after two additional attempts, it started to purr.

I wriggled my hips and settled in, leaned back, and closed my eyes. I'd watched Suzy park this car in the school lot every day of senior year. When she left for lunches, she made no secret of her departure. Occasionally, I spotted the car around town, each time wondering where she was headed.

Again, I was struck by how little I knew about what her life was like. If at one time we were two girls from Ribbon High, then somewhere along the line our lives had diverged significantly. I couldn't deny the circumstances that put her in that prison for life, yet, she maintained the same outward appearance of calm as she had back in the twelfth grade.

I climbed out of the car and shut the door behind me.

"You want me to bring my car around back?" Eddie asked.

"No. I want you to help me get those cardboard file boxes into the trunk."

"You're taking the car?"

"I can't stop thinking about what it would be like to be Suzy Kintz. Driving her car is a start."

CHAPTER 23

On Loan From a Friend

By the time I got home, it was dark. We were a week before Daylight Savings, and March still felt like winter. Nick was at the dining room table. He was surrounded by leather and fabric swatches, and a stack of invoices sat to his left. I set down a box of files and kissed him hello.

"You've had a long day," he said.

"Looks like you have too."

He nodded. "I might be up for a collaboration with Vitamin P," he said. "Last-minute opportunity that could mean a lot of publicity."

I dropped into the seat across from him. "You're collaborating with a vitamin?"

"Vitamin P is a hip-hop artist." He smiled. "Your personal playlist may be filled with the Go-Go's, but to the rest of the world, he's a big deal."

"Then I hope he sees you're a big deal too." I stood up. "Do you mind if I move your truck? I brought home some files, and I want to unload them in the garage."

"Sure," he said. "Keys are in the bowl."

The house where Nick and I lived had at one time belonged to my parents. When the deed changed hands (along with a humble sum and a grand amount of stress), they packed up and moved to Southern California and left behind the stuff people accumulate through life. I rid myself of the greatest collection of half-empty paint cans in Pennsylvania, several broken lawn chairs, and a dozen green garden hoses. I stacked the hand-me-down tools and garden supplies under the workbench and on top of the shelves, and vowed to use the garage as a garage, not storage.

I moved Nick's truck to the street out front, left the dealer SUV in the driveway, and parked the Cabriolet in the garage. I moved the truck back to the driveway. I went in the garage and shut the door so that to any random detectives who might be interested in my whereabouts, things at the Kidd-Taylor house were just like any other day.

"What's that?" Nick asked from the doorway. He pointed to the car.

"It's a 1994 Audi Cabriolet," I said.

"Did you buy it?"

"No. It's on loan."

He raised his eyebrows. "It doesn't have dealer plates."

"It's on loan from a friend."

"Have I met this friend?"

"No. She's staying at a — a private resort." I fumbled with the words.

Nick crossed his arms. The amber light from the garage sparkled against the face of his watch. He leaned against the door frame, and his expression was one of amusement, not concern.

"It's Suzy Kintz's car," I confessed. Once the admission was out, the words kept coming. "She used to drive it in high school. She told me I could use anything I needed. I need a car, and it was right there, and — do you think it was wrong for me to borrow it?"

By now, Nick had left the doorway and entered the garage. He peered into the back seat. I hadn't been able to unlock the trunk, so the cardboard boxes lined the backseat.

"Files," I said. "They were at the house, but the electricity was off so I couldn't go through them while I was there. And there's more."

"More files?"

"No. More information. Loncar. He's working for Conrad Vega. He was asking questions at the pretzel store earlier today." I turned and stared at the closed garage door. "I'm his competition."

"Kidd, don't take this the wrong way, but I don't think Detective Loncar considers you his competition."

"Well, he should. I'm very resourceful." I pointed to the back seat of the car. "I've got reporters from competing papers working together, and access to her case files. The governor's office said it doesn't matter how many deathbed confessions exonerate Suzy, she's never getting out of jail. And why would Conrad Vega hire Loncar anyway? Is he hoping to find new evidence or bury it? I could be looking at a massive cover-up."

Nick helped me carry the boxes inside the house and upstairs to the spare bedroom. He'd wanted to turn it into a home office, but sharing space with my off-season wardrobe had turned out to be distracting. Now he worked at the dining room table or at his office.

It took four trips to get the boxes inside and up the stairs. Logan oversaw the process by sitting on the second floor landing and meowing each time one of us rounded the corner. On the final trip, I found him bent over a carton, sniffing the files. "There's nothing for you in there," I said. I picked him up and scratched his tummy, kissed his head, and set him down a few feet away. He returned to the same box and this time swatted a piece of torn paper that stuck out the top.

"No, Logan," I said.

He got onto his hind legs and started chewing on the folder edges. I snatched the file from the box and set it on my desk. He looked longingly at it and then at me and meowed as if stating his discontent with the situation. I scooped him up again and this time carried him to the kitchen, where I gave him a handful of kitty treats. My parenting skills hadn't developed much past the bribe stage, which both Logan and I accepted.

"Have you eaten?" Nick asked. He stood by the counter with his phone in his hand. "I was thinking of ordering hoagies."

"I had a hoagie for lunch," I said. "How about a pizza?"

"It's a good thing you're active," he said while dialing.

I let Nick handle the ordering and picking up of the pizza. Truth be told, I was more interested in taking a bite out of the files I'd brought home than in takeout. I was long past the curious stage, and while the files I brought home might not contain a blow-by-blow account of what happened, they'd contain the source of public opinion, and I probably needed to know that too. I climbed the stairs and opened the file on the desk.

It was filled with clippings from various publications: the *Ribbon Eagle*, the *Philadelphia Post*, the *New York Times*, and more. I fanned them out and then, not wanting to wait another minute, picked up the first one and read. And three hours later, with the pizza Nick had brought back totally forgotten, I had a better idea of what had happened that night and exactly how hard it was going to be to disprove what people thought.

CHAPTER 24
Kind of Zen

WHEN NICK CAME TO CHECK ON ME, I WAS JOTTING details onto index cards and thumbtacking them to the wall. (This was how they handled investigation on the Hallmark Channel mysteries, and with Loncar out of the picture, I had to turn elsewhere for investigation advice.) (They didn't thumbtack directly into the walls, but Nick and I had been discussing paint colors, and that meant spackle was in our future.)

"You've been quiet up here," he said. He stared at the wall. "And busy."

"Is there any chance you're up for a break? I could use a sounding board."

"I'll listen, but I can't promise I'll be your most alert partner."

"You'll do in a pinch," I said with a smile.

He checked his watch. "Come to the kitchen. We'll hash it out over cold pizza."

I followed Nick downstairs and put a room-temperature slice of pizza onto a plate. He poured me a glass of Pellegrino and sat across from me. I swallowed two bites and then set the slice down, drank half of the glass of water, and started my recap.

"The police found Trenton Vega's body, shot twice, at the Kintz residence at one-thirty a.m. on Thanksgiving morning. He was pronounced dead at the scene. His blood alcohol level was point two one —"

"Point two one? Do you mean point one two?"

"No. Point two one. It's in the toxicology report. Way past the legal limit. There were some other substances in his bloodstream, too. Trenton Vega liked to party." I pushed my chair away from the table. "This might be easier if we go back upstairs."

"Go on up. I'll be there in a minute," Nick said, leaving me vaguely confused. Unlike Trenton, Nick did not like to party. He enjoyed martinis when relaxing and was down for wine with dinner but didn't even like taking cold medication. A few minutes later, he entered with two mugs of coffee. He handed me one and sipped from the other. "This'll help."

I took the mug and inhaled then set it on my desk. "When's the last time you inhaled the scent of coffee?"

"Just now."

"I don't mean because it's there. I mean to just stop and inhale and think about the fact that you are in the presence of coffee, that your decision to drink or not drink is totally up to you. To think about where the coffee came from and what you had to go through to get it."

"Is this about daily gratitude? Did you rehire your life coach?"

"Suzy Kintz inhales one drag from a cigarette every day.

She lights it, inhales, exhales, puts it out, and then tosses the pack."

"Sounds a little affected."

"I watched her do it. She said when the smoke enters her body, she's aware that she's breathing, and when she puts the cigarette out, she's aware that she's in control over what happens to her. It's kind of Zen."

"You're not considering her as your new life coach, are you?" Nick asked with a note of concern.

"I just think maybe being more aware of what we do, and what we have control over, is not a bad idea."

Nick crossed the room and set his coffee down next to mine. "Come here," he said. I turned to him, and he wrapped his arms around me and kissed my forehead. "You believe her, don't you?"

"I do," I said into his shirt.

He rested his bristly cheek on top of my head. "I don't always love the situations you get yourself in, but I love your heart." He kissed the top of my head and then pulled away and looked me in the eyes. "The caffeine is doing its job. Walk me through what you got."

Nick sat in my chair, and I stood by the wall. "Like I said, Trenton Vega was pretty out of it when he died. Two bullet wounds, lots of blood. The bullets were retrieved from the scene and were matched to a Sig Sauer P239, which just so happened to be the same type of gun Suzy bought him when he told her he was worried about a client."

"She shot him with the gun she gave him. Is that significant?"

"I don't know yet. She told me about the gun today. She

said her family always had guns, so she wasn't worried about having one in the house. She bought it for him for self-defense. When they came here for Thanksgiving, he brought it with him."

"I don't want to get ahead of you, but are you sure it's the same gun?"

"No. The police were, and the defense was, and the jury too, but I'm not."

"Go on."

I picked up a new index card and flipped it against my fingertips. "Suzy had been out to dinner. Her statement says she took a shower when she got home, and when she came out of the bathroom and found her husband dead on the floor, she called the police. She says she didn't hear anything." I tacked the card to the wall. "It's the same thing she told me this week. Her story has never changed."

"Seems hard to believe."

"There's a blood test on her too. She was at point oh nine, which is just past the legal limit. She admits she took a Valium before dinner. She was stressed about spending time with people she hadn't seen in years."

"The shower seems suspicious."

"She said she showered to get the smell of smoke out of her hair before bed."

Nick tipped his head from side to side as if weighing the conflicting accounts. "It's plausible," he acknowledged. "Everything she says is plausible, but it also sounds convenient."

"The police claim she got drunk to work up her nerve and then she shot him and showered to get the gunshot residue off. They think she took the Valium to calm down after she realized she killed him."

"That sounds plausible too. What else?"

I shrugged. "That's most of it. The crime happened in the early morning on Thanksgiving day. The courts were closed for the holiday weekend. Normally, the police can only detain someone for twenty-four hours before they need a signed arrest warrant, but because it was Thanksgiving weekend, they had Friday, Saturday, and Sunday too."

"Let me guess. By the time they got to the judge, they had the evidence they needed."

"Yep. The warrant was signed on Sunday night. This was classic rural justice. The murder took place on the outskirts of Ribbon. It was an election year, so it looked good for them to act fast. The facts fit their narrative, so they didn't bother looking for any other possible answers."

"It's possible the police were right," he said. "Rural justice or not, the evidence fits. She says she knows guns, and she handpicked that one for a reason. She might not have been thinking clearly, and she can't account for her whereabouts within a range of certainty. There were no witnesses and no evidence to support that anyone else was in the house."

"And yet, would she use the gun she bought him if it could be that easy to prove she bought it for him? She was thinking clearly enough to end her night early instead of staying out with the group. There was nothing in the house that seemed to indicate any struggle. She found his body and called the police. She left everything untouched until they got there." I tapped an open file. "It even says here that she was in a terrycloth robe when the police arrived. She didn't even get dressed."

"Maybe she thought that would buy her some leniency."

"Suzy Kintz wasn't like that."

"Kidd, I know you went to school with her, but are you the same person you were in high school?"

"Not even close," I said.

"That's right. Maybe Suzy's life after high school set her on a course where that night was inevitable."

I considered what Suzy had told me about her life post-high school. She'd left Ribbon the night of graduation, married Trenton a year later. Three years after that, she was convicted of murder. She sat in a local jail for two years awaiting her trial, and by the time she was convicted, I'd finished four years of college and started working for Bentley's. Her life was over and mine had just begun.

"I've been through all of this, and I haven't found a motive." I closed the file folder on the desk and ran my fingertips over a piece of clear tape on the back. The tape appeared to have held something on the file, but over time, it split in two. I leaned down closer and recognized the faint outline of — was that what I thought it was?

I dropped down on all fours and pulled the partially empty cardboard box of files closer to me.

"What's wrong?" Nick asked.

I held my hand up in the air to hold off any additional questions and then grabbed the remaining files in the box and stacked them on the floor. When the files were removed, one thing was left in the bottom of the box.

I reached in and extracted a tarnished brass key. An

attached tag was labeled with a unit letter and number, not unlike the storage locker I'd put my belongings in when I visited the prison. I held the key up. "Suzy told me her things were moved into a storage locker. Her family didn't know anything about it, but it seems like her lawyer did." I pulled the key closer and stared at it. "I wonder what else he knows."

CHAPTER 25
A Local Nancy Drew

Brewster & Case was a legal firm that handled clients at a certain financial level. They had a solid reputation as an ethical firm, and their cases won far exceeded their cases lost. Suzy had fallen on the wrong side of the equation, but she'd never threatened to fire them or demand new representation. Even my dealings with them had been efficient, and I had no reason to believe they were in on a conspiracy against her. Still, I went into their offices with my eyes wide open.

"Samantha Kidd to see Mr. Brewster," I said to the receptionist.

The door to the offices opened, and a middle-aged man came out. "Ms. Kidd?" he asked.

I nodded. "Call me Samantha."

"Bill Brewster," he said. We shook hands. "Follow me."

We walked down a carpeted hallway and ended our two-person parade in his office. It was a study in wood: desk, walls, table, chairs. The office supply budget must have a line item for Murphy Oil.

I sat in a chair opposite his desk and set my handbag on the chair next to me. I hadn't been able to shake the idea of pretzel style, so today I dressed in a warm brown knit fit-and-flare dress with a brown-and-white polka-dotted scarf tied at my neck.

Bill awkwardly lowered himself into the chair behind the desk. He opened the middle drawer and pulled out a bottle of aspirin. "Back injury," he said. He shook two tablets into his palm and swallowed them with a sparkling water chaser. "I was hoping we'd get a chance to meet. You visited with Ms. Kintz at the Correctional Facility last week, right? How is she?"

"I haven't seen her since high school graduation, so I might not be the best judge of her mental state."

"Suzy hasn't approved a visitor since she's been inside. I assumed the two of you were close."

"Not exactly. I don't think anybody in high school knew her very well."

He looked troubled by this, but not so much so that he explored the circumstances of our relationship. "Nevertheless, I considered it a good sign when she asked me to make the arrangements. You're on her approved visitor list indefinitely, so if this is about continuing to meet with her, it was unnecessary."

I pulled the key out of my handbag and set it on his desk. "I'm here about this," I said. I kept my fingertips on the tag with the identifying unit number. "My most recent visit with Suzy was cut short. I had to leave unexpectedly, and Suzy seemed shaken. She told me about a storage locker. Is this the key?"

"Ms. Kidd, I understand you're something of a local

Nancy Drew, but if you weren't friends with Ms. Kintz, then why do you care? What do you expect to get out of helping her?"

It wasn't an inappropriate question. It was one that had been lingering at the back of my brain for days, and I hadn't yet worked out the answer. Was I doing this for Suzy? And if so, why? We might have been friendly from time to time, but we hadn't been friends. This was hardly the basis for us to start sharing nail polish and talking about boys. Was I doing all of this to make myself feel good — an act of altruism that confirmed I was a good person despite my sometimes-selfish tendencies? And if I were doing this for me, wasn't that selfish too?

"Free pretzels for life?" I offered as a potential answer.

He smiled. "Well played." He looked at the key. "May I?" he asked.

I slid the key toward him. He picked it up and held the tag away from the key and stared at the tarnished brass. He appeared to understand that this wasn't just any key. I fought every impulse to ask him what he knew about it.

"Where did you find it?" he asked.

"In the bottom of a cardboard box filled with Suzy's case files. Her sister said your office sent over the files about five years ago, and they've been in the guest cottage ever since. I've been feeling a little manipulated over the whole thing, so I read them last night to try to understand what happened that night."

"What have you learned?"

"That Suzy's statement was probably the biggest piece of evidence against her."

He nodded. "That is the sad truth."

The longer I sat across from Bill, the more I wanted to talk about her case. One thing in particular had been troubling me from the get-go. "The confession from the prisoner at Rikers came out of nowhere." I remembered what the man at Tanner Auto had said about Suzy arranging a payoff for him to claim his involvement. "Is there a connection between the two of them? Did he know her?"

"After his confession, the prisoner gave notarized testimony that matched evidence at the scene that the investigating officers never released to the public. He willingly submitted to a DNA test, and it matched with skin swabbed from under the hiker's fingernails. The prisoner confessed to six additional murders, all unsolved, and provided information to corroborate his statement. There's no doubt that he killed the hiker."

"Could he have killed Trenton Vega?"

Bill shook his head. "There's no connection and no evidence. The police questioned him extensively about it and he didn't even know the Kintz compound was close."

I shifted weight in the chair and asked what I couldn't shake. "Do you think Suzy did it?"

He seemed unsurprised by the question. "I have no reason to believe she didn't." He set the key down halfway between us. "That was the problem. Suzy said she didn't do it, and our firm argued that she didn't do it, but in the end, we had nothing to prove she didn't do it. No evidence to support that someone else came into the house and shot him. Nothing to help tell an alternate story. Do I think she did it? No. But can I prove that with the evidence at hand? No. And that, Samantha, is why Suzy Kintz is in jail. Not because she did it, but because I could not prove that she did not."

I didn't pick up the key, but I gestured toward it. "Do you know where the storage unit is?"

"Route 222. When she was arrested, I maintained the payments on her apartment in New York until after the trial, but after the guilty conviction, the situation required a more permanent solution."

"What's in the locker?"

"Clothes, shoes, handbags, that sort of thing. Trenton and Suzy both did a fair amount of entertaining in their respective lines of work, so there are chairs, glassware, bar carts."

"Don't most people rent those things?"

"Rental fees add up. Suzy asked me to make the arrangements for the property to be stored. We were hopeful that she'd be out after the trial, and my firm thought it best to also remove anything that would remind her of that night."

"But Suzy didn't get out after the trial."

"No, she did not." He sighed. "After the murder, it became cheaper to have Suzy's possessions moved from New York to Pennsylvania and stored here."

"Now that a prisoner from Rikers confessed to the second murder that was linked to Suzy, what are the chances of her getting a second trial or getting out on parole?"

"There is no parole in Pennsylvania. Not unless Suzy can demonstrate a violation of her constitutional rights."

"But she's serving two consecutive life sentences based on that second victim, and thanks to the prisoner confession, it's now known that she didn't do it. Her sentence should be commuted."

"That decision is in the hands of the governor, and in this case, I don't see how he's going to be cooperative."

I remembered the hostility I'd gotten from the governor's office when I called, and again questioned why. "I don't get it. Why would the governor want to keep her locked up for life if she's not guilty?"

"A lot of people think the governor got elected because of how he handled Suzy's case. It was a high-profile murder investigation that gave Berks County national exposure. His son's the governor now, and admitting his dad was wrong, even for a small part of that case, opens the door to a reexamination of the evidence, a possible retrial, and a lot of questions. At the minimum, it undermines both of their leadership."

"The governor would rather leave an innocent woman behind bars to protect his position of power and his dad's reputation?"

"Leave the governor to me. I've got connections in high places, and if you can prove Suzy Kintz is innocent, public opinion will be the least of the governor's problems."

CHAPTER 26
This Meant Something

It was close to lunch by the time I left the offices of Brewster & Case. I stopped at a convenience store and picked up a copy of the *Philadelphia Post*. Joey's most recent installment in the Vega murder series was called "Cocktails before Murder," and included the court transcripts from the restaurant staff from night of the crime. I tossed the newspaper on the passenger seat to read when I wasn't operating heavy machinery and tore into the bag of Kintz pretzels and ate two. Crumbs clung to my scarf. I dusted them off. (The benefit of driving a car owned by a pretzel heiress, even if she was in prison, was that pretzel crumbs were probably not a big deal. The benefit of dressing in pretzel-inspired style was that crumbs blended in.)

I drove to Suzy's storage locker. It felt strange, driving her car, going to explore her belongings. Like I was *Single White Female*-ing her. Considering I'd tried to keep my fascination with her under wraps in high school, it was odd to make it public now.

I pulled into the parking lot and circled the units until I found the one labeled "C." Security cameras were mounted on each of the buildings, and I parked somewhere between the two closest, either staying out of range or ensuring that I'd be on both. I locked the car and went to the unit, where I had trouble with the lock. I lubed the key with a blob of vanilla-scented lip gloss and worked it into the lock until, after several minutes of jiggling, the lock popped open. I pulled the door up and took in the contents.

I'm not sure what I expected to find inside, but it wasn't this. The left was filled with stacks of plastic ghost chairs on square dollies. The back of the unit held metal rolling rods with clear plastic garment bags. I stepped farther inside the locker to examine the clothes. The garments inside were all designer items, some still with the tags attached. I counted the garment bags on the bar and multiplied by the number of bars . . . there had to be more than a hundred.

This could get distracting.

Now that I was inside the storage locker, I continued my big-picture inventory. Cardboard cartons were stacked along the right wall. They'd been sealed with tape from a packing gun. I peeled the tape back and revealed cartons of shoe boxes. Gucci, Prada, Blahnik, Roger Vivier, Jimmy Choo, and even Nick Taylor. Suzy and I did not share a shoe size, but that didn't stop me from pulling on a pair of white knee-high boots that were two sizes too big and looking around for a reflective surface.

After Suzy adopted her uniform of white T-shirt, black suit, and Gucci loafers, aside from red-carpet events, she'd never been photographed in anything else. The amount of merchandise inside the storage locker that still had tags attached suggested the designers she interacted with didn't accept defeat easily. Garment bag after garment bag held samples that had been messengered to Suzy at *Luxe*. She'd had a world of designer labels at her disposal, but still, she maintained her own style.

I slipped into a cream wool coat trimmed in faux fur that looked so real I had to double-check the tag and a pair of gold-rimmed sunglasses. The act was psychological; I wanted to get inside Suzy's head. I was already driving her car. Why not wear her clothes too?

I pulled a cranberry felt derby hat over my hair to ward off the chill and flipped through the garment bags. I removed three and draped them over a chair by the door. It was hard to imagine designers had been this munificent to the editor of *Luxe*, the small magazine Suzy edited, but when I got to the second rack and discovered magazine pages clipped to individual outfits, I realized that wasn't what this was about. Suzy's vast wardrobe had less to do with her role at *Luxe* than her role as Trenton Vega's wife. She appeared with him at all sorts of music industry events. These were designer hopefuls who understood the power of giving Trenton Vega's wife an outfit in the hopes it would be photographed.

On the end of the rack hung a garment that had been dry cleaned. It was inside a clear plastic garment bag like the others, but the dry-cleaning plastic was still over the clothes, and the hanger was wire covered with paper. I would have liked to know which dry cleaner Suzy trusted with her designer wardrobe, but the attached piece of paper was a generic hand-written slip with the word "Rush" scrawled across it in ballpoint pen.

The outfit inside was a two-piece white dress. The top had a funnel neck and bracelet sleeves, and the matching pencil skirt was long and narrow. It was an ensemble you wore with extreme confidence. Head-to-toe white was a magnet for stains. I had a feeling this outfit saw the dry cleaner more than most people saw their dentists.

I pulled the garment bag off the rack and unzipped it so I could get a better look at the receipt. There was a note from the cleaner about a stubborn stain. I removed the garments and held them up. The light from outside was waning, and it was difficult to see details, but the surface of the luxurious ivory knit appeared to be unmarred. As I was putting the garments back into the plastic, I was able to make out the dates on the ticket.

It had been dropped off at the cleaners the day after the murder.

I felt a familiar sensation inside my bones that radiated outward and made me both hot and cold at the same time. It was my inner radar sending up a warning flag. This meant something.

I lifted a ghost chair off a stack and placed it on the ground and then sat in it to think. There had to be a plausible explanation. Obviously someone else had access to the storage locker. For starters, her lawyer did. He'd been in possession of the key. I imagined a narrative where the dry cleaner called to let Suzy know her cleaning was ready, but that wasn't how it worked. When she dropped items off, they'd tell her the date to pick them up. I knew from Joey's article that she'd been taken in for questioning the morning of the murder, detained over the weekend, and a judge had signed off on her warrant before the sun came up on

Monday. Suzy Kintz had gone from shower to holding cell in twenty-four hours. She hadn't had time to make a side trip to the dry cleaners.

There was another question that came out of the discovery of the dry-cleaned outfit: why. Once Suzy left that house, she hadn't come back. *Why* would someone have her garments cleaned? And why a rush job? Suzy had sat in that jail for two years, awaiting her trial. This outfit had been taken to the cleaners the day after the murders. There were no other items listed on the receipt. What made this outfit so special?

A growing suspicion blossomed inside me. I had to find out if what I suspected was right. What I needed was to talk to someone who could tell me what Suzy had been wearing the night Trenton Vega died.

I already knew there was a dearth of information about Suzy's case on the internet. Aside from a couple of newspaper articles that had been scanned in and were difficult to read and blogs of true-crime fans who had added her to their databases, there was little to find. The archived files that I had at home contained police reports, statements, and additional clippings from Suzy's arrest and conviction. I couldn't even dig through her Facebook profile for a picture that commemorated that night, because social media hadn't even been a thing at the time. Most people didn't even trust the internet yet.

I pulled my phone out of my handbag and called Carl.

"Collins," he answered.

"Carl, it's Samantha Kidd. I need you to check a fact for me."

"Fact checking isn't my job," he said. "Call research." He hung up.

I shook my head and called him back. "Don't hang up," I said when he answered. "I'm in Suzy Kintz's storage locker out on Route 222. There's an outfit here that was —" I stared at the outfit. This was ridiculous.

"That was what?" he asked. "If this is a question for your style column, I'm going to the editor to demand that your pay gets cut in half."

"Carl, wait. This might be important. I need to know what Suzy Kintz wore to dinner the night Trenton Vega was murdered."

Carl was quiet for a moment, which was an improvement over hanging up on me. When he spoke, it was in a conspiratorial tone. "Why?"

There was no point in keeping info from Carl if I wanted his help. "I found an outfit that was taken to the dry cleaner's the day after the murder. It was marked as a rush job and picked up the Monday that Suzy's arrest was official. It might mean nothing, but I can't figure out why someone would take her cleaning in on the day after the murder."

"Hold on."

I held the phone to my head and waited for Carl to return. About a minute later, he came back. "There's nothing online about what Suzy was wearing that night."

"Call Joey Carducci. He's doing a series on the case. He might know."

"You want me to call another reporter?"

I tried my argument about Woodward and Bernstein again to no avail. "I have Joey's card in my handbag. I could have called him myself, but you made a very strong case about loyalty and the brotherhood of journalism. Remember?"

"This goes against everything I believe in," he said, and then begrudgingly added, "I'll conference him in."

The phone went silent and about ten seconds later, the call waiting beeped. I didn't recognize the number. I accidentally hung up on Carl while answering.

"Hello?" I answered.

"Samantha Kidd? Joey Carducci from the *Post*. Collins called me. Said you want to know about Suzy Kintz's outfit the night of the murder."

"Yes. Do you know what she was wearing?" My heartbeat pounded in my neck, my chest, and my toes. If Joey did and Carl didn't, then Carl's call could have simply let Joey know how much of a scoop the *Post* had.

"Hold on while I conference in Collins." The phone went silent again, and a few seconds later both reporters were in on the conversation. "Kidd, Collins says you're in Suzy Kintz's storage locker. What did you find?"

I hesitated for a moment, staring at the outfit and wondering if I could trust Joey. "I'm staring at an outfit that was sent to the dry cleaners the day after the murder and marked as a rush job."

"I don't know what happened to her clothes. She was wearing a bathrobe when she was taken into custody."

"If this is the outfit Suzy wore to dinner, then it might be significant."

"Good work," Joey said. "Give me the address."

"You're in Philadelphia," Carl said. "I'll handle this. Stay there, Kidd, I'm on my way."

"We're working this story together," Joey countered.

I rolled my eyes. "You two can hash out your by-line later. Carl, you have an editorial meeting this afternoon. I'll finish up here."

"Be careful, Kidd. That outfit might be more important than you know," Carl said.

"It's under two layers of plastic. Nothing's getting to this thing."

"Collins is right," Joey added. "If someone else put that outfit in the storage locker, then you're not the only one who knows it's there."

CHAPTER 27
Practically the Same

YOU KNOW THAT FEELING YOU GET WHEN YOU THINK you're just going about your day, doing what normal people do, and suddenly feel super exposed? Like the world was black and white and you were dressed as a traffic cone? That was me. I'd been happily digging around Suzy's things while the door to the storage locker was wide open. I'd heard cars driving around and hadn't stopped to consider that, while other people might be going through their belongings, I was going through those of a convicted felon.

Perhaps I should try to do things on the down low.

I found a light switch inside the storage unit and flipped it. I hadn't needed it with the exterior light, but after what Joey said, I thought it prudent to close the door. I eased the door down. Before it shut completely, a familiar car pulled into the lot. It was Detective Loncar's dark-gray sedan.

I slammed the door to the ground and stepped to the side of it. There was no locking mechanism on the inside of the locker, which I suppose made sense if you thought about storage lockers from the perspective of the person who rented them and not the person hiding inside. But if Loncar knew which unit was Suzy's, he could simply open the gate. And what would I say when he found me inside? Surprise?

It didn't matter. I had a key. It wasn't like I was breaking and entering. I was simply following a lead, the same as him, and I'd beaten him by a couple of hours. Considering he was the professional investigator, he was the one who should be worried about what to say to me.

I remained in the ghost chair, not wanting to make a sound. A few minutes later, I heard footsteps on gravel. Two male voices accompanied them. "This is the unit," one voice said. "Rent gets paid every month like clockwork. That's all that matters to me."

"You haven't seen anybody come in here recently?" This was Loncar. "Maybe today?"

"I'll be honest. I don't much pay attention to this unit. It was rented when I started working here."

"What would it take to get inside?" Loncar asked.

"Warrant from the police," the man said. "Doesn't matter how long it's gone unattended. When people rent from us, they expect privacy and security. We don't take that responsibility lightly. If you don't have a key, you're not getting in."

"You don't keep a master on file?" Loncar asked. "What happens if someone locks themselves out?"

"It's their responsibility. A locksmith can handle it, but that's on the tenant, not on us."

I sat still, listening to the conversation on the other side of the metal door, wondering when Loncar was going to notice that the padlock was missing. It wasn't a stretch to think he would. All he had to do was grab the handle and yank up and he'd find me, wearing Suzy Kintz's fur-trimmed coat and oversized glasses like a four-year-old playing in Mommy's closet.

Could he do that? Maybe not. In the past, Loncar could have waved his badge and asked the owner to open the unit, but now, he was a private citizen with a business card. Just like me.

My business cards had pictures of dresses and shoes on them, but other than that, we were practically the same.

There were two knocks on the metal door, which I hadn't anticipated. I jumped. My phone fell from my lap and landed on the ground. It made a thud. I sat perfectly still, listening for signs that one of them had heard me.

"Mice," the employee said. "Maybe rats. After all these years, who knows what's in there."

"Right," Loncar said slowly. "Can you give me a moment? I need to make a call."

"Sure," the employee said.

Go away, go away, go away, I repeated inside my head. I quietly pulled my feet up to my chest and hugged my knees. My cell phone rang. Crap! I scooped the phone from the ground and switched the ringer to silent right about when I saw the caller's name: Loncar.

Damn detective Loncar and his investigative skills!

A moment after the incoming call disconnected, Loncar spoke again. "There's a car parked at the end of the lot. White Audi convertible. Is that yours?"

"Nope. That one comes every couple of months."

Every couple of months? That made no sense.

Except it made all kinds of sense. That car didn't drive like a car that had been sitting abandoned for seventeen years. Someone had been driving it. And whoever had driven it had brought it here. That meant this locker hadn't been abandoned for all this time, and either the employee knew that and was giving Loncar the brush-off, or he was ignorant.

Another possibility existed. That the person driving Suzy's car had rented a separate storage locker in this unit. Maybe this one had gone untouched, but if we could get our hands on a list of renters and cross-reference it to a list of people who knew Suzy, then maybe we'd find a common name. Like in *The Thomas Crowne Affair*. Eddie and I often argued over which version was better, but I maintained that you just couldn't top Rene Russo's wardrobe in the remake.

But if Loncar couldn't get the storage facility to open the unit, then how was he going to get a list of renters? That was as much of a violation of privacy as getting inside the unit without permission. And it also implied that Loncar would work with me, and the last time I checked, we were playing Spy vs. Spy.

I listened as the men's footsteps faded, and then stood up and crept toward the door. A few seconds later, I heard the sound of a car engine and then tires on gravel. I had no way of confirming if that was Loncar's car or someone else's, but just in case, I'd give him time before I left.

I sat in the chair and stared at the garment bag with the white outfit. I couldn't help feeling like I was on to something. I hadn't been afraid to meet with Suzy the first time because the last time I'd seen her, she hadn't been accused of murder, and my brain, filled with nostalgia, couldn't justify that fact into the mental file of what I knew about her. But for the first time since meeting with her, I felt like maybe those indisputable facts could be dismantled with new evidence that told a different story.

I picked up my phone and called Suzy's lawyer. "Samantha Kidd calling for Bill Brewster," I said to the receptionist. "It's urgent."

She put me through to Bill's office.

"Samantha," Bill said. "I was just about to call you."

"Great minds think alike," I said. "I'm at the storage locker, and I found something. An outfit from the dry cleaner. It looks like it was dropped off the day after the murder. I'm going to ask Suzy about it the next time I visit her. I think it could mean—"

"I'm sorry, Samantha. I have bad news. I heard from the prison today. Your visitation privileges have been revoked."

"They can't do that! Suzy didn't do anything wrong. I didn't do anything wrong. This is a conspiracy. Somebody doesn't want her talking."

"It's not the prison. It's her. Suzy changed your visitation status to denied."

CHAPTER 28
Worn Out My Usefulness

I SUDDENLY FELT COLD ALL OVER. "WHY WOULD SHE DO that?" I asked. "The last time I was there, she asked for my help."

"Did something happen during that visit?" Bill asked.

I thought back. "We were interrupted. The guard came over and told me I broke the rules and I had to leave. It was because my friend who gave me a ride got out of his car and was wandering around outside the prison."

"That may be what happened that day, but this is different. This was Suzy's choice."

"I have to talk to her."

"Samantha, I appreciate your interest in my client's case, but this isn't up to you. I trust you understand the seriousness of this matter. Don't jeopardize Suzy's chances at clemency by showing up at the prison and making a scene."

Everything about this felt wrong, from the dry-cleaning tag to Suzy canceling my visitation rights. I'd been lured into this, and now I was being cast out, like a trend that finds itself moved from the "Hot" list to the "Not." I appeared to have worn out my usefulness.

That indicated I'd accomplished something, though to me it felt as if I was not far from where I'd started.

I gathered the garment bags from the pile I'd made and put them back on the rack, all but the one with the white outfit. The novelty of wearing Suzy's unworn designer gratis was gone. Whatever had motivated her to get me to the prison that first day had changed, and now I was no different than any other member of the public, a resident of a killer's hometown willing to spin theories on what had happened that fateful night.

I carried the clear garment bag out of the storage unit and locked it up behind me. The parking lot was deserted. When I reached the car, I tried the trunk again. This time I wriggled the key back and forth until it finally popped open.

The trunk wasn't empty. Inside was a flat metal lockbox. My hands shook as I pulled it closer to me. I flipped through the keys on Suzy's keyring and found a small round one that slipped into the lock. It turned. I lifted the lid and found the box filled with bound stacks of hundred-dollar bills.

"Excuse me!" called a male voice.

I closed the lockbox and slammed the trunk shut. A man approached me. I tightened my grip on the keys and stepped around the side of the car to the driver's side door. I raised my arm in a half wave and climbed inside.

Of the choice between peeling out or hearing what the man had to say, one had the potential to yield information. I buckled my seatbelt and drove forward, slowing when I reached him.

The man bent down to my window. I unrolled it a few inches. He looked in, first at me and then around the interior of the car, and then back to me. "Have I seen you around here before?" I placed his voice as the one talking to Loncar while I was inside the storage unit.

"I don't know," I said honestly. I've found, in situations like this where the urge to lie is tempting, it's best to remain vague.

"Which one of these units is yours?" he asked, moving his finger around to point at the various lockers.

"None," I said. I added, "I'm doing a favor for a friend."

He looked past me to the back seat. "You must have been dropping off," he said.

I shrugged and smiled. "People don't like to get rid of things anymore," I said. "I suppose that's the foundation of your business model."

He chuckled. "Is this your car?" He tapped the roof.

The longer he kept me there, the more I wanted to leave. It hadn't been that long ago that he and Loncar had been outside Suzy's storage locker. What if Loncar hadn't left? What if he'd just pulled his car around the back row and parked? He had to know I was inside — that ringing phone trick confirmed it. And now, I had the biggest clue that I'd found to date in the trunk of Suzy's car.

The phrase "sitting duck" came to mind.

The phrase "turn the tables" followed shortly thereafter.

"I was supposed to meet someone out here but he never showed," I said. "Older man, balding, sloped shoulders, orthopedic shoes? Probably was wearing a plaid shirt?"

The employee straightened up and stared out across the

lot. "He was here. Asking questions about C-10. That's not your friend's unit, was it?"

I pretended not to have heard him. "Is it four thirty?" I asked. "I'm late for an appointment. Nice talking to you!" I rolled up the window. This time, peeling out of the lot was the only option.

I drove home and parked the Cabriolet in the garage. I had to get the SUV back to the dealer, but first, I wanted to find out what was in that metal box.

I carried the dry cleaning and the lockbox inside, up the stairs, to my makeshift war room. I hung the clothes in the closet between a fake fur coat and an old band uniform and set the box on the desk. The locking mechanism hadn't closed properly, so I jammed the key between the narrow opening and jimmied it until the lid flopped back.

The box contained stacks of money. Each bundle held fifty hundred-dollar bills. I counted seven rows of ten stacks. A quick calculation tallied up to around thirty grand. It was a significant sum in terms of money-in-a-trunk, but not in terms of the-car-owner-is-wealthy. I dug below the cash and found a folder containing photos from a fashion shoot for *Luxe Magazine*. The discovery gave the money context; this must have been work-related.

The outside of the envelope had been dated and stamped PAID IN FULL prior to Suzy's incarceration. Initials on multiple lines confirmed photo approval. It appeared to be a similar process to what we'd used for advertising back when I was a buyer and we signed off on proofs for an ad campaign.

The envelope was partially sealed, most likely the result of moisture seeping into the lock box over time and making the pre-glued envelope tacky. I slipped a letter opener into the side opening and slid it at an angle then tipped the envelope and extracted the glossy images. They were exactly what I'd suspected: images from a photo shoot. Ten images in all, followed by a contact sheet that had been marked up with a wax pencil indicating the images the magazine intended to use. I flipped the top photo over and saw a stamp on the back: *property of Luxe Magazine.*

What had seemed like a clue had turned out to be a piece of unfinished work business. These photos would have likely appeared in an upcoming issue of the magazine, sometime after the murders. Instead, the magazine had enjoyed a brief moment of fame when Suzy was arrested, and then languished, eventually being pulled from newsstands and pulped to make room for the next hot trend. Old issues sold on eBay for little more than the original cover price. Crime sure didn't pay for Suzy.

I lined up the bottom edges of the glossy pages and started to put them back how I'd found them when I discovered a white business-sized envelope that hadn't fallen out when I thought I'd emptied the packet. "Contract" had been written on the envelope in ballpoint pen. I looked inside and found not a contract as expected, but an incident report that documented a case of domestic abuse.

There were things I knew how to do, and research was one of them. Digging through the archives, delving into how to make a risqué video, badgering people until they spilled their secrets, and sometimes relying on plain old luck. I didn't have the first idea what to do with a partially completed police report.

But I knew someone who did.

CHAPTER 29

Applicant to the Cult of Wrongful Justice

I READ WHAT HAD BEEN DOCUMENTED. IT WAS FROM the 12th Precinct in New York. The report was partially completed, but from the details present, I gleaned pertinent information. The date was the same year as the murder, six months prior. The name of both victim and suspect had been left blank, and the report hadn't been signed. It wasn't a stretch to believe the victim was Suzy and the abuser had been her husband. They didn't call it domestic abuse for nothing. I wondered if this was a one-time thing, or if it had been a pattern in the Vega household. I'd heard nothing about it.

It seemed unlikely to me that someone who'd excelled at art classes, who'd shown me the proper way to use eyeshadow, who'd been born into a family that made pretzels and managed an indie fashion magazine, could have ever been capable of the crime of which she'd been convicted. But now, I had to consider it.

One of the few things she'd told me on my first visit was

that Trenton Vega was not a nice man. Had she been trying to tell me something? Or was this another breadcrumb to lead me to piece together a narrative that had somehow not been included in her trial?

Suzy Kintz left school every day for lunch, and no one ever knew where she went. She'd been kicked out of three prep schools and eventually enrolled in Ribbon High with the instructions to graduate or go without her trust fund. She'd left town that night, disappeared for years, and then turned back up with an edgy job and a media mogul husband.

I dropped into the chair behind my desk and called Detective Loncar. He answered on the second ring. "Hi," I said. I hadn't talked to Loncar in days, and before I confided in him, I addressed some unfinished business. "Did you come to my house and unplug my electric car?"

"Who is this?"

As if he didn't know.

"It's Samantha Kidd." I gave him a moment, but he didn't respond to my accusation. "Forget about the car. I found something, and I think it's important, but I don't know because I don't have access to the same things you do. If I told you what it was, would you look it up for me? A favor for a friend?" Again, I was met with silence. "Or you could consider me an anonymous source calling with a tip and look it up yourself."

"You already identified yourself."

"You know what I mean. You're working for Conrad Vega, right? If someone had information about his son's murder, you'd check it out. I know you would. Don't write off valuable intel because you think I don't know stuff."

"I know you know"—he paused—"stuff."

"Damn straight I know stuff." I looked at the partially completed police report. "Except I don't know if Suzy Kintz is innocent."

"What's the favor?"

"See if there were any partially completed domestic violence incident reports in the 12th precinct in Greenwich Village about seventeen or eighteen years ago."

"That's awfully specific."

I stared at the incomplete incident report. "And yet, it's completely vague at the same time."

"I'll see what I can do." He hung up.

I needed to go over the facts again, but this time, I wanted to see if I could tell a different story. I spent the next hour covering seventeen pages in my notebook with a plot that could have made the *New York Times* bestseller list.

The crime: murder.

The victim: Trenton Vega.

The weapon: Sig Sauer P239.

The motive: escape from an abusive and controlling husband.

The alibi: dinner with friends. The excuse of stress and Valium to fog Suzy's memory. Smoking, drinking, car service home to blur her alibi. The shower to remove gunshot residue before calling the police. It was the case that had been argued.

Geri Loncar had said people called her "Boozy Suzy" because she could hold her liquor. Maybe the too-drunk-to-drive excuse had been an act. Maybe her BAC was the result of alcohol consumption after she pulled the trigger.

If the incident report that I'd found with the money had

been used as evidence, it might have made a jury sympathetic to her. But I went back through the case file and found no mentions of Trenton Vega as having tendencies toward violence.

I stood up and pulled the garment bag out of the closet. This time, I opened the bag and then removed the dry-cleaner plastic. The note mentioned a stubborn red wine stain, but again, I found no discoloration marring the surface of the garment. This was ivory ponte knit. It seemed close to unbelievable that even the most talented dry cleaner would be able to get a red wine stain out of ivory knit.

Red wine.

Something about that bothered me, but it took a moment to realize what. It was something I'd read in one of the *Post* articles. I searched my email for the zip file from Joey and quickly found the one with the quote from the waiter. "It sounded like New Year's Eve," he'd said. "They were popping corks every ten minutes."

Assuming the waiter had nothing to hide, then it begged the question: where did the red wine come from?

What if the dry-cleaner note was fake? What if I was meant to find it — Suzy had to know I'd go through her clothes — and use it as the clue on which to hinge her new trial? I couldn't get a clear picture in my head, but the more I considered every fact in front of me, the more I questioned whether they were facts at all.

You don't leave a man like Trenton Vega without a plan. Suzy's words came back to me. Like everything else I'd discovered today, they felt like a carefully conceived nugget to lead me down the very path I'd followed. I felt like an applicant to the cult of wrongful justice and Suzy was my leader.

I called Suzy's lawyer. It was a little after six, and the odds of him being at his desk were fifty-fifty.

"Bill Brewster," he answered.

I identified myself. "This isn't about visitation," I added quickly. "I'm working on a story for the paper, and I have a question about Suzy's case, and I thought you might have the information there."

"I thought Carl was on crime?"

"It's a fashion story. A puff piece." Great, Samantha. In what world did reporters write puff pieces about convicted felons?

"What's your question?"

"What happened to the outfit Suzy was wearing the night of the murder?"

"She was wearing a bathrobe when she was arrested."

"Not then. Before. When she was out to dinner. The timeline says she murdered her husband and then took a shower, so I figure she was still dressed when she murdered him and took her clothes off after."

"Oh, yes. The police collected her clothes as evidence. They couldn't prove if there was any gunshot residue on her because she showered, so they wanted to determine if there was any GSR on the clothes."

"Was there?" I asked.

He was silent for a moment. "Yes," he said finally.

I wasn't nearly as surprised by that as I was by the white outfit hanging in front of me. "That means they sent the clothes to a lab, right? What would have happened to them afterwards?"

"They'd be sealed and put into an evidence locker. Property of the state. If Suzy gets a retrial, our biggest challenge is going to be invalidating the conclusions of those technicians."

CHAPTER 30
Not Going According to Plan

I THANKED BILL AND HUNG UP, BUT I DIDN'T MOVE. I sat in the chair and stared at the ivory outfit in front of me.

It was going to be close to impossible to figure out anything about this outfit. Seventeen years ago, it might have been on the cover of some retailer's catalog, but aside from purchasing back copies from every retailer in a twenty-mile radius of New York City on eBay, I wasn't going to find out much. And even if I did discover the stores that carried it, they surely didn't maintain their client purchase files for decades.

Someone had taken the garments to the dry cleaner after she was arrested, and then put them in storage. They had told the cleaners there was a red wine stain on the garment, though the cleaners couldn't locate the stain in question. Why would they say there was a stain if there wasn't?

I'd once spilled wine on a pair of jersey trousers. My hopes of salvaging the garment had been minimal, but I asked my dry cleaner nonetheless. He said there would be a twenty-dollar surcharge for stain pretreatment, to which I agreed. When I picked up the garment, I was shocked to find it in pristine condition.

When met with my open admiration for his work, he boasted that he soaked them in club soda for twenty-four hours, which dissolved the stain (and made him a tidy profit from the twenty dollar surcharge!). His wife had joked that club soda was their secret weapon, and he told his wife if she kept telling the customers, it wouldn't be a secret anymore. I promised not to tell, though I started stocking club soda and treating wine stains myself.

The dry-cleaner tag had listed the pre-treatment and the cleaning fees separately. I figured it was a function of their system: whatever services I was paying for would print out on the ticket and receipt, just like this one. So, was that what this was all about? If this were a brand-new garment, it would look like a brand-new garment. But with the tags torn off, the dry-cleaner tag noting special treatment, the clear plastic and the flimsy metal hanger, it made the garments appear preowned.

I called Bill back. This time, he didn't answer. I left a brief message. "Bill, this is Samantha Kidd again. I need to know who else has access to Suzy's storage locker." I left my number even though he probably had it in any number of places and hung up. Until I heard from him, the ivory outfit was a dead end.

I closed the files and left the room. My brain was on overload. I needed to think about something other than murder and pretzels and high school, and there was one pretty big thing that I could think about that had nothing to do with any of those things: the sex tape I would use to make Nick famous.

Nick was due home in an hour. I still wasn't sure how I was going to lure him to the bedroom and position him in front of the camera, and to be honest, I was starting to lose my nerve. But this wasn't about me; it was for Nick's business. If there was one thing I had learned through my recent investigation, it was that scandal was good for business.

Maybe I should wear a wig?

I changed out of my brown and white pretzel outfit and into a pair of thigh-high stockings and a black lace night-gown. A layer of temporary pretzel puff bulged over the waistband of my panties.

Maybe I should trade my thigh-high stockings for Spanx?

I checked the placement of the camera, hidden between a row of books I'd carefully placed on the dresser a week ago. The battery was still at 100%. I turned and looked at the bed. It looked too neat. I threw the covers back and got inside and rolled from side to side to make it look more natural. I got back up and looked at it again. Now it just looked messy. I made the bed again and smoothed my hand over the duvet cover.

Maybe I needed a glass of wine?

I went downstairs and fed Logan and then checked the fridge for an open bottle of wine. We had champagne. I pulled a bottle out and cut through the foil while my hands shook. I should have anticipated this. I should have picked up something earlier today, maybe on my way home from the storage locker.

I popped the champagne and filled a flute then took a

sip and closed my eyes while the bubbles tickled my tongue. The front door opened, and Nick called out, "Kidd? I'm home early."

He came into the kitchen. I was frozen in place, with the bottle of champagne in one hand and my flute in the other. I'd all but forgotten my racy black lace ensemble until his eyes swept over me from head to toe and back. They stopped somewhere around my muffin top.

"You look . . ." He came closer. He put his hands on my hips and nuzzled my neck. "Great."

My brain fired warning shots at me like a Revolutionary War soldier at a redcoat. We were in the wrong room. I hadn't checked my makeup. And it wasn't like I could do much to participate, considering both of my hands were full.

"Not here," I said. I leaned away from him.

"Why not?" he said. He kissed me, slow and gentle, and for the briefest moment, I thought *why not?* myself. And then I remembered the plan. "Upstairs," I said.

"You've got to learn to be more spontaneous," he said. His hands, unencumbered by a champagne bottle and a flute, found other activities, which made it more difficult for me to concentrate.

I tipped my head back and focused on a spot on the ceiling so as not to get distracted. I could excuse myself and go upstairs. Get the camera and sneak it back down. Hide it by the coffee maker. Yes. That could work. Maybe not the coffee maker. That side of the kitchen didn't have good light. Maybe I could wedge it between the blender and the Ninja Foodie 5-in-1.

I stepped away from Nick and handed him the champagne flute. "For you," I said. "I'll be right back."

I set the bottle down and started to leave. Nick reached for my wrist, but I pulled away quickly. I kissed the tip of my index finger and touched his lips. "Hold my place," I said.

I rounded the corner and took the stairs two at time, which was a mistake. I reached the landing out of breath. Logan was curled up on the middle of the freshly made bed. Small dents in the duvet cover remained where his paws had been. "You're lucky the plan changed," I told him. I didn't see any way I could explain bringing the Diva Light Ring to the kitchen, so I unclipped the burner phone and keyed in my unlock code. If I started recording now, I just had to place it once I reached the kitchen —

"Kidd, what are you doing?" Nick asked.

I whirled around, and the hem of my nightie caught on the Diva Light Ring stand. It fell over with a clatter against the wooden bureau. I turned away from Nick to pick it up.

"Leave it."

I straightened and faced him. "I can explain," I said.

His eyes moved from the tipped light ring stand to the burner phone in my hand. He slowly turned his head from the spot where the light ring had been to the side of the bedroom where the light ring had been aimed: the bed. Logan stood up and walked to the edge of the bed and jumped down then left us alone.

Things were not going according to plan. Nick was in the bedroom and the bed was available, but I'd just dismantled the camera!

"What is this?" he asked. He took the phone from my

hand. The camera app was recording. "You were going to record us? Without talking about it first?"

"I'm making a risqué recording," I said. "For you. For your business."

"For my *what?*"

"Scandal is good," I said defensively. "You'll have instant name recognition. This will solve your publicity problems!" But even as I said the words, I knew this was among my less-good ideas. Nick glared at me, and there was nothing in his expression that indicated he still thought my problem-solving instincts were charming. "I had a whole plan," I added.

"I can't handle this right now," he said. He yanked the drawer to his dresser open and grabbed some clothes, shoved them into an overnight bag, and stormed out of the room. Seconds later, the front door opened and slammed, and seconds after that, Nick's white pickup truck backed out of my driveway and took off down the street.

CHAPTER 31

A Disaster

I raced after him. "Nick!" I called out. It was a waste of breath. His taillights disappeared at the end of the street when he turned left.

Everything I'd been preoccupied with left my mind, replaced by one thought: catch up to Nick and apologize. I grabbed a coat from the hall closet and pulled it on over my sexy ensemble, grabbed Suzy's keychain and my handbag, and left.

I was getting more comfortable driving the Cabriolet, and in seconds, I was on the street, going the direction Nick had driven. He had enough of a head start that I couldn't see him, but it was late, and I hoped the lack of traffic would make his white pickup truck easier to spot.

I drove first to his showroom, a small retail space in the middle of a strip mall that was less than two miles from my house. It was the easy choice, and Nick would know if I were looking for him that this was the first place I'd go. The lights were out, and his truck wasn't in the lot.

I circled the lot, hoping to find him out back in the loading zone, but succeeded only in wasting valuable follow-that-car time. I pulled back out on the highway and drove aimlessly, scanning the streets in search of my husband.

Nick had always supported my plans, and this time, it was a plan we would do together. I'd found a way to help, and I'd wanted it to be a surprise. And the whole idea had blown up in my face.

Without thinking too much about it, I followed the road through downtown Ribbon, got on the highway, and headed north. I exited by the apartment building where Nick Senior lived, and I struck out again. The Maserati was gone.

It was the final straw in a row of final straws. I pulled into Nick Senior's space and cut the engine and rested my head on the steering wheel. I felt numb.

A sex tape? What had I been thinking? I didn't even like sitting around the doctor's office in a paper gown. How exactly had I expected to leak it? And to whom? I didn't have a distribution plan. Aside from a couple of websites I feared had compromised the search history on my laptop, I didn't even know what to do with the recording once I made it. My plan had been a disaster.

Scandal and publicity. Two concepts I'd latched onto from Suzy's case. But the key players in her world were either dead or incarcerated. The increased exposure might have made Trenton Vega rich, but he wasn't around to enjoy his wealth. And Suzy might be the most famous graduate of Ribbon High, but from the cheap seats, it didn't appear as though fame was doing her or her family's company any good either.

I closed my eyes and let all the energy drain out of me. I was exhausted, and for nothing. I wasn't a true crime reporter. What was I going to discover that Carl or Joey wouldn't get to first? And who did I think I was, pretending I could outsmart Detective Loncar and two reporters who'd been doing this for the better part of their adult lives?

I felt around on the passenger seat for my handbag and pulled out my phone. In my haste to leave, I'd grabbed the burner. I left it in the cupholder and rooted around some more until I found mine. I tapped the screen and called Carl. He didn't answer.

"Carl, it's Samantha. The story is yours. I have boxes of files at my house and access to Suzy's storage locker. Let me know what the best way is to hand it all over to you." I hung up.

My next call was to Bill. It was after hours, so I was more prepared for his machine. "Bill, this is Samantha Kidd. I've turned everything I have over to Carl Collins at the *Ribbon Eagle*. He'll do more for Suzy than I ever could. Can you arrange for him to get visitation rights? I think it would be good if he and Suzy talked one-on-one."

I disconnected a second time and held my phone. In two phone calls, I'd given up control of the biggest thing in my life, and I felt exactly the same. There was no sense of loss. I tapped the Recents list of incoming calls and saw Nick's name over and over and over, and I felt an ache in my chest as if someone had hit the Off switch to my heart. I ran my thumb over the screen as if touching his name was a connection.

I needed to talk to him, to apologize to him, to explain. No, that was wrong. I didn't need to try to make him understand anything. Nick's business was Nick's business. He knew what he was doing and didn't need my help. My "help," rooted in innocence and good intentions as it always was, complicated his life in ways I hadn't ever stopped to see.

As I swiped my thumb up and down over the touch screen, the phone connected to his number and started to ring. In self-help circles, there's the belief that there are no accidents, so I didn't hang up. The phone rang one time, two times, three—

And then there was a knock on my window. I jumped. Outside the car, Nick's dad stood with a phone in his hand. He gestured for me to roll down the window.

"He's not here," Senior said.

"Where is he?"

"I don't know. He parked out back and took the Maserati."

"Is that his phone?" I asked, pointing at Senior's hand.

"Yes."

"He doesn't want to talk to me," I said in a shaky voice. "I messed everything up."

"Come inside, kiddo. I don't know what you did this time, but it'll blow over like it always does."

I turned off the engine and buttoned my coat while following Senior into his apartment. (Wouldn't want the neighbors to think Nick's dad hired a professional!)

Since Nick moved out, Senior had gradually personalized the apartment. A brown leather sofa sat facing a big-screen TV. Copies of *Kiplinger's Personal Finance* magazine and *Hemmings Muscle Machines* were neatly stacked on the bottom level of the walnut end table. A coaster with a pilsner that was two-thirds filled with a pale ale sat on the coffee table next to the *New York Times*. The walls were bare, save for a small oil painting done by a local artist that hung on the far wall.

A wave of heat enveloped me. I stuck my finger between the collar of my coat and my neck and pulled the fabric away from my skin.

"Take your coat off and stay awhile," Senior said.

"I — I can't. I'm not dressed for a social call."

Senior stepped away and scanned me. The only parts of my ensemble that weren't visible were my sheer black stockings and heels. "He wasn't kidding," Senior said.

"He told you?"

"He didn't have to spell it out. I haven't seen my boy that flustered since the footwear models used to flirt with him when he was thirteen." He shook his head. "You're a piece of work, I'll give you that." He turned away and then looked over his shoulder. "Follow me."

We walked through the living room to the room that used to be Nick's. Inside, Senior opened the third drawer on an armoire and pulled out two gray garments. "Change into these and come on back out. I'll put on a pot of coffee."

I changed out of the black lace nightie and stockings and into a pair of gray cotton sweats not unlike the ones Suzy wore at the prison. They felt appropriate; I was starting to see how badly I'd violated Nick's trust with my plan and felt like I deserved a prison sentence myself. I folded my nightie and stockings up into a pile the size of a dinner napkin and tucked it into the inside pocket of my handbag.

I left the room and rejoined Senior in the kitchen. Bardot

stood on the floor by his feet, looking up. Her pointy black ears quivered in anticipation of peanut butter. Nick Senior sliced a spoon through the smooth surface of a jar of Jiffy then held the spoon toward the French bulldog's head. She made snorting noises while she licked the spoon clean. She hovered by his feet while he filled two mugs with coffee. I followed Nick Senior to the living room and sat in the middle of the black leather sofa; he eased into the La-Z-Boy chair that bore the signs of being his favorite. Bardot climbed up a small dog stool next to the La-Z-Boy and curled up in Nick Senior's lap.

"I was trying to help—"

Senior cut me off. "You're always trying to help." He took a sip and then set his cup on the coffee table. "You help people because it makes you feel good, right? Let me ask you something. How do you think that makes the people in your life feel? That you're always helping them and they never get a chance to help you?"

"That's not how it is!" I protested. "Nick helps me all the time. There was the surveillance on the mall, and the time I had to stay at a motel, and when the police brought me in for questioning, and Vegas —"

He held up his hand. "That's not helping you. That's being your assistant. I'm talking about the unconditional love and support you get from the people in your life who aren't paying you to clock in. They're just there. How do you think those people feel knowing there's nothing you can't do for yourself?"

"It's not like that," I said. Half the time I felt like more of a mess than a Mississippi Mud Pie. "I know I have control issues, but I'm working on them."

"How?"

"What?"

"How are you working on them? Have you talked to anyone? A professional?"

"My life coach and I are on a break."

"So . . . therapist? Shrink? Stranger on a train?" He set his mug down on the end table and stroked Bardot's head. The puppy closed her eyes and relaxed.

"I'm more into self-help these days." I waited for a comment. Most people have something to say about that. But he just sat there watching me, as if he were waiting for me to talk. "Podcasts and books, stuff I can listen to when I'm alone in the car. I bought Air Pods so I could listen around the house and not distract Nick when he's there. I think it's working. It's hard to say since it's just me doing the work."

Oh.

Nick Senior was right. I didn't let anybody help me. Even my personal growth had become a solo venture, something I believed I could do without assistance. My vulnerability was about as accessible as the Berks County Correctional Facility for Females, and I'd denied entry to everyone in my life.

"I don't know how to fix this," I finally said.

"Junior is upset. Not just because of what you did, but because he's frustrated. This is a man who lost everything and is starting from scratch. He needs to feel some control over his destiny, and despite your best intentions, you're sending signals that you don't need him. You have to give him time to figure out that whatever cockamamie plan you hatched that has you dressing like Sophia Loren is probably more good than bad."

"Did he . . . tell you what I did that made him so mad?" I asked tentatively.

"Let's just say there are some things that should remain between a husband and wife." He winked.

CHAPTER 32
Sleeping Alone

I wanted to spend the night. I wanted to curl up in Nick's old bedroom, under Nick's old blankets, in one of Nick's old T-shirts. But if everything Nick's dad said was true, then sooner or later, Nick was going to return with the Maserati, and my presence at his dad's might undermine my new resolve to mind my own business.

I drove home. After I removed all filming and lighting equipment from the bedroom, I went to the kitchen and cleaned up the champagne then went to the office and powered down the computer. I left the gray sweats and sexy sleepwear on the bed and took a long shower. I dressed in non-sexy cotton pajamas and crawled into bed. Logan joined me. I stared at the ceiling for hours, not wanting to accept that plans to make a sex tape had led to me sleeping alone.

———

THE NEXT MORNING, with no phone calls from Nick, I was depressed. He'd claimed to like the part of me that helped people who didn't ask for my help, but his hostile departure indicated otherwise. I'd wanted him to be happy. I'd wanted him to thank me. It was one more indicator that my efforts on his behalf hadn't been on his behalf at all. Like a lot of our life, they'd been all about me.

Sometimes, being me was more exhausting than the local news.

I'd slept on wet hair, which left my hair looking crazy. I pulled it back into a low ponytail and pulled on underwear then stared in my closet, trying to decide what to wear. But everything in there reminded me of me, and I was the one person I wanted to escape.

I left my bedroom and went to the office, where the ivory outfit hung. It wasn't evidence. Suzy's lawyer had confirmed that the outfit from the dinner party was still in police custody.

I tore off the dry-cleaner plastic and put it on. Ponte knit was not the sort of fabric I was accustomed to wearing without a layer of spandex shapewear underneath, so I stripped it off, pulled on some shapewear to smooth out my pretzel puff, and slipped the outfit back on. I added white knee-high boots and moved my things into a white handbag, buckled on my pink-faced Rolex, and left. I drove straight to the closest Walk-ins-Welcome salon and entered.

"Do you have an appointment?" the receptionist asked.

"No, but I have a wallet full of cash and a strong desire to see someone different when I look in the mirror."

"Follow me. I'll get you shampooed."

———

THE SALON GAVE me the distraction I needed. The stylist cut my hair into a bob and lightened the ends so the effect was black roots to white tips. A makeup artist had suggested a berry-colored lipstick, which stood out in stark contrast to my pale skin. I picked up a pair of tinted aviator sunglasses from a rack by the door and added them to my tab then tipped a healthy thirty percent on top of the total. I left the salon with several new best friends.

I got into the Cabriolet. I looked different (which I knew from the reflection in the car windows as I approached), and more importantly, I felt different. I drove to the coffee shop and went inside. Heads turned toward me. A flush of insecurities came up, but instincts I didn't know I had tuned them out.

"What can I get you?" the woman behind the counter asked.

I'd been to this coffee shop twice a week for years and always ordered a large coffee. "Small no foam latte," I said. "With an extra shot of espresso."

"Anything else?"

I scanned the case of baked goods. My stomach was still knotted over Nick and my fight, and even a fancy makeover couldn't make me forget the temporary pretzel puff around my waistline. "No, thanks."

She rang me up, and I waited until my beverage was brewed. I felt people watching me, but I did my thing. When my drink was ready, I carried it out of the shop to my car and left. I drove to a nearby automatic car wash and relaxed against the leather seats, enjoying my morning jolt of caffeine while giant rollers buffed and polished the exterior of the white car.

These weren't the choices I normally made, yet I was making them today. Latte? Espresso? Car wash? And as for my hair, I'd once taken scissors to it myself and then called Eddie to fix. Salon cuts and colors weren't part of my routine.

After the blowers finished drying the car, I pulled into traffic. I drove toward the paper. Halfway there, I realized what I was doing. I wasn't making decisions as me, I was making them as a stranger. It started with the car.

When you read enough self-help books, you start to notice that they all say the same thing. Start with a small change in your life, and from that small change, a snowball effect of change will follow. If you want to see things differently, you have to change your mind. This isn't the same as wanting pizza for dinner and then, moments later, wanting a hoagie instead. It's a process where you create new neuropathways in your brain. Eddie's tired of hearing me talk about it. He says the only reason I care is because it makes me sound smart.

(I *am* smart. I married a shoe designer, didn't I?)

I've always been a little afraid of changing my mind. I mean, it's my mind, you know? It's the thing that has solved homicide cases when the police couldn't. It's what helped me land on my feet after being accused of killing my boss. It's how I dealt with almost running out of money and losing the house, and helped a friend when someone murdered her husband, and found a colleague who'd been kidnapped, and all sorts of things. You don't just figure those things out if your mind isn't doing something right.

And what if my mind and the way I think was the best thing I've got going? What if that's why Nick loved me, why Eddie hung out with me, why Loncar tolerated me? What if I changed my mind and turned out to be like everybody else?

The familiar anxiety I always felt when thinking about things like this returned, but instead of cranking the volume on the radio, I sat with my feelings. I let the anxiety rise up until it almost engulfed me. The car felt hot, and the air felt prickly. I adjusted the rearview mirror and caught my reflection. A jolt of unfamiliarity interrupted my anxiety.

Who was I kidding? I'd changed my mind the moment I got behind the wheel of Suzy's car. It was as if a piece of her transferred to me, her confidence, her privacy, and her detachment from the events around her. It was what the papers all wrote about when her case was in the daily news: she showed no remorse. It was just like high school when she left for lunch period and nobody stopped her. She didn't spend her time helping other people; she was untouchable.

And the truth was, I liked how that felt.

I tightened my hands on the steering wheel, and I knew where I needed to go.

I passed the exit for the paper and drove to Brewster & Case. Bill hadn't returned my second call from last night, but that wasn't going to deter me from getting answers. I parked out front and went directly to his law offices. The receptionist was on the phone. She didn't seem to recognize me. "Please hold," she said into the phone. "May I help you?" she asked me.

"Yes. I'm here to see Bill Brewster," I said.

The receptionist clicked her mouse and checked her screen. I assumed she was looking at his schedule.

"We spoke late last night. He may not have added it to his calendar." I smiled and then moved away from her desk toward Bill's office. She hadn't granted me permission to enter, and I didn't even know if he was there. But whatever momentum I'd picked up from my borrowed confidence propelled me forward. I put my hand on the doorknob and turned. And as the door eased open, I heard Bill's voice.

"She called me again last night. She found something in the storage locker." He was quiet for a moment. "She called back with questions about evidence. She can't go back to the prison, but she's not going away."

It was clear Bill was talking about me, but who was on the other end of that call? I hadn't considered for one moment that Suzy's lawyer was not to be trusted, but that was exactly how it sounded.

I pulled the door shut quietly and turned to face the receptionist. "On second thought, maybe I'll use your ladies' room first."

CHAPTER 33

A Reasonable Explanation

FLEEING TO THE RESTROOM WASN'T THE MOST WELL-thought-out decision I'd made, but I had to collect my thoughts. I hadn't told the receptionist my name, but she'd met me once before, and it was a matter of time before she buzzed Bill and told him I was there.

Maybe I'd misunderstood. Maybe the half of the conversation I'd overheard hadn't been about me. The rational part of my brain calmly observed that Bill was a criminal defense attorney, and he probably had more than one client who approved and denied visitation requests, but the irrational part of my brain, the part with the neuropathways that needed to be overridden, believed to my core that I was the she he discussed. And if Bill was talking about me, then who was on the other end of that phone call?

I ran my wrists under cool water to collect myself. I'd been about to enter Bill's office when I heard that conversation, and fear of being caught turned me away. But maybe fear could work to my advantage. Maybe I wasn't the one who should be worried in this situation. Bill had something to hide, and I'd never know what it was if I left.

I dried off my hands and left the restroom. The door to Bill's office was open, and light spilled out onto the carpet in the hallway. I didn't turn to check if the receptionist was watching me. I tapped my knuckles on the door and stepped inside. The receptionist hadn't been watching me from her desk because she was seated in a chair in front of Bill's.

"Mr. Brewster," I said. "Thank you for agreeing to see me on such short notice." (I've found, when you're forcing the hand of someone who may have something to hide, it's often valuable to flat-out lie.)

Bill kept his eyes on me but turned his head toward his receptionist. "Thank you. We'll pick back up when I'm finished here."

The receptionist vacated the chair, and I stood back to give her room to leave. After she was out of the office, Bill said, "Close the door."

I gently eased the door shut but remained standing. "You seem surprised to see me," I said.

"Where did you get that outfit?" he asked.

I'd hoped to see the color drain from his face, or beads of sweat to pepper his hairline. If this were an Adrian Lyne movie, he might even demand I take it off. But Bill showed nothing more than curiosity, like a child who recognizes that one of these things is not like the other.

"It was in Suzy's storage locker," I said. "The one that the key unlocked." Having played the outfit card as well as I could, I approached one of the chairs in front of Bill's desk and sat down. "I took it yesterday. It had a dry-cleaning tag dated the day after the murder. You confirmed to me that the outfit Suzy was wearing the night her husband was killed was collected as evidence, tested, and stored in a secure facility, and she said I could take whatever I wanted out of the locker, so I thought it was fair game. The one thing I can't figure out was why did someone rush to have it cleaned?"

"The Kintz family had a standing dry-cleaning pickup every Friday," Bill said. "That was Thanksgiving week, so the clothes didn't get picked up until Monday. The dry cleaner back-dated the order and put a rush on the job so the clothes would still be ready for Tuesday pickup."

"But Suzy was detained over the weekend, and by Tuesday, she was arrested."

Bill nodded. "Whoever picked up the clothes hung that with the rest of Suzy's clothes. When I arranged for her things to go to the storage unit, everything she had was moved."

It made sense. A reasonable explanation for something I'd wanted to believe was significant. Now, I was right back where I started. Except –

"Did you know Suzy was abused?" I asked. I pulled out the partially completed domestic abuse report. "It seems like she changed her mind about filing a report, but if it happened once, it might have happened more than once, and if it happened more than once, it might make her sympathetic to a jury if she gets a retrial."

Bill pressed a button his phone. "Is my ten o'clock here yet?"

"Yes, he just arrived."

"Great. Send him in." He sat back in his chair.

I leaned forward. "Your ten o'clock can wait. This is

important. You need to file an injunction or petition for a retrial or whatever it is you do in cases like this. Contact the Innocence Project. Leak a story to the media."

"Aren't you the media?" asked a voice behind me.

I stood up and found myself face to face with Bill's ten o'clock: Detective Loncar.

"What are you doing here?" I asked. I turned back to Bill. "Are you cooperating with him?"

Bill looked at me then at Loncar. This time there was no mistaking the confusion on his face. He addressed Loncar. "I thought you told me Ms. Kidd worked for you?"

"You what?" I asked. I mean, Loncar telling people I worked for him was something of an endorsement, but I couldn't help feeling like he'd leveraged our relationship for his own gain. (Which was a little like helping him without even knowing it! But we're not going to get distracted by that.)

Loncar, to his credit, didn't flinch under interrogation. The room filled with tension as the three of us remained silent, each waiting for someone else to speak.

I took the time to notice what Detective Loncar was wearing. Since going into the PI business, he'd expanded his daily wardrobe from ill-fitting suits with orthopedic shoes or plaid shirts and Wranglers to whatever it took to blend in with his surroundings.

On a recent case where we *did* work together, I'd arranged for Nick's dad to let him borrow some clothes so he looked the part of business investor. It appeared as though he hadn't yet returned the loan. Today he wore a chocolate-brown turtleneck and dark denim jeans over brown suede loafers. To anyone who didn't know better,

Loncar looked like he knew his way around a department store. To me, he looked like he wanted people to think he was something he wasn't. Maybe he was trying to create new neuropathways too.

I shifted my attention to Loncar's face. He was watching me. He was waiting for me to react. Whatever I said or did would determine his next move. My whole morning had been a series of doing things differently than I had in the past, and the cumulative effect of that much change made my next move easy.

"I guess we got our signals crossed," I said. "But since we both cleared our schedules, we might as well hear what Bill has to say about Suzy Kintz's case." I turned away from Loncar and sat back down. I turned and looked back at him. "Or if you prefer, you can go back to the office, and I'll talk to Bill myself."

CHAPTER 34
A Gutsy Choice

I smiled. Loncar frowned. Bill waited.

"Mr. Brewster, can you give me a moment alone with my colleague?" Loncar said.

"Use my conference room," Bill said. He pointed to the door. "Across the hall."

I followed Loncar to the vacant room and crossed my arms. "Well?"

"I looked into what you asked. Eighteen years ago, a woman who'd been severely beaten filed a domestic abuse charge at the 12th precinct in Greenwich village, New York. She said she was in a car accident, but the injuries didn't fit. When one officer suggested she'd been attacked and asked her to press charges, she took the paperwork and left. The officer wrote up a separate incident report and filed it so there would be a record if she came back. The dates and description line up with what you told me." He hesitated. "How did you know about this?"

"I found a copy of the partially completed incident report with Suzy's things," I said. I paused a moment and then added, "It was buried under thirty thousand dollars in cash in a lockbox in her trunk." If anybody was going to listen to me, it was Loncar. "She may have been planning to leave him. Thirty grand isn't a huge amount of money to a person like either one of them, but it might be enough cash to allow her to split and stay off the radar if he tried to find her."

Loncar nodded slowly, as if this wasn't my worst theory. "The money came from Conrad Vega."

"Trenton's dad? The man who hired you to look into this case?"

"Yes. Suzy told him about the attack and said she wanted out of the marriage. She said either Conrad would help her, or she would publish the incident report in her magazine and destroy the Vega name. He said he offered her half a million dollars for the incident report so he could ensure it never got out, but she refused."

"She didn't need the money, but going to her husband's dad was a gutsy choice. Almost like she was putting the family on warning." I furrowed my brow. "Conrad Vega hired you to look into his son's death, right? Now that you know this, do you think Suzy killed him?"

This time, his hesitation lasted longer. "No," he finally said. The hesitation indicated he wasn't sure.

Loncar turned to leave and I stopped him. "When I got here, Bill was talking about me with someone on the phone. He mentioned me losing visitation privileges and the evidence I found in the storage locker."

"You don't know who was on the phone?"

"I was hoping it was you."

Loncar shook his head.

"Could it have been Conrad Vega? If he offered Suzy half a million dollars back then and hired you now, he might try other avenues too."

"I won't rule it out."

We returned to Bill's office. Bill sat behind his desk pouring steaming hot coffee into his mug. Two empty mugs sat on the opposite side of his desk in front of the chairs.

"Coffee?" Bill asked. He held up the pot. Loncar and I both nodded. He stood and leaned over, filling both mugs, and then turned and sat the pot on a hot plate. He lifted his mug and drank, making a slurping noise in the process. Loncar did the same (sans slurp). When neither men showed signs of having been poisoned, I assumed the coffee was safe to drink.

I wrapped my hands around the mug and blew on the surface while I thought about what Loncar had told me. The involvement of Trenton Vega's dad complicated my theories about Suzy's behavior, as did the money in her trunk. It seemed as though she'd been gearing up to leave her marriage, but then why did she change her mind?

In that moment, I knew Suzy had lied about that night. Was it possible that they hadn't planned to arrive separately at the Kintz family compound, but that she'd left first and he'd shown up unexpectedly? Had she shot him in self-defense, or worse, as a shortcut to reclaim her freedom? Or was the separate arrival part of the plan and she hired someone to commit the crime for her? Was her innocent shower a convenient excuse to be out of the way while someone else did the dirty work? I had to confront her with this new information. It was the only way to let her know I didn't automatically believe everything she said.

"Why did Suzy revoke my visitation privileges?" I asked.

"I was contacted by the prison after your most recent visit. Suzy, who has been a model prisoner for seventeen years, had an altercation."

"An altercation?" Loncar asked.

"A fight with another prisoner."

"What did the prison do about it?" I asked.

"Suzy was put into solitary confinement for seven days."

"But it hasn't been seven days since my visit," I said. "How could she tell them to revoke my privileges?"

"Prisoners in solitary don't get visitors," Loncar said.

I looked back and forth between their faces. "You told me Suzy revoked my privileges. That meant she didn't want to talk to me anymore. That's not what happened. You lied to me."

"Suzy's actions required necessary disciplinary action from the prison. She knew that those actions would result in her losing visitation rights. That is the language that came from the prison. It wasn't until I called back to arrange my visit that I found out what had happened."

"Why would she get into a fight?" I asked. "After all this time, why would she do something to make her circumstances worse? She's gone seventeen years with no hope of getting out, and now she has hope. Why screw it up?"

"Maybe Suzy Kintz is exactly where she should be," Loncar said.

"Can you visit her?" I asked Bill.

"I'm her lawyer. It's a different class of visit. I'm scheduled to go in the day after her solitary confinement ends."

"What about Carl Collins from the *Ribbon Eagle?* I left

a message last night asking you to arrange for him to see Suzy."

"I left a message with Mr. Collins. He needs to provide me with some background information just like you did. Until he returns my call, I'm at a standstill on that request."

"Would you excuse me?" I said. I stood, grabbed my handbag, and stepped into the hallway.

Carl not jumping on the Get Into Jail Free Card didn't make sense. He'd been hammering me about this case since the day he found out I got inside to see Suzy. I could accept that Nick needed time to work through whatever issues I'd triggered when he saw the sex film setup, but Carl wasn't that complicated. Hand him a scoop, and he'll shovel his way to the story.

I pulled out my phone and called him again. The call went straight to voicemail. "Carl, it's Samantha. You need to get in touch with Bill Brewster at Brewster & Case Legal Firm. He'll make arrangements for you to get in to see Suzy, but you have to give him some background info first. Call me back when you get this."

I hung up and called Joey Carducci. The last time I'd talked to either one of them had been from the storage facility.

"Nice town you got here," Joey said. It was less popular than "Hello," but he was from Philly, so I gave him a pass.

"Joey? This is Samantha Kidd from the *Ribbon Eagle*."

"I know who it is. I have caller ID like the rest of the world. Did you talk to Collins? Whatever he said is a lie."

"I haven't heard from Carl since yesterday. That's why I'm calling. Did something happen?" There was silence on the other end of the phone. "Joey? Are you still there?"

"Hold up. You mean Collins didn't call you last night?"

"No. Why? Did you guys figure something out?"

"Yeah. We figured out neither one of us plays well with others."

"Joey, I've had a long night and a long morning, and I'm not in the mood for games. What happened after we got off the phone yesterday? Where is Carl?"

"You want to know what happened? I drove up from Philly because you convinced me to collaborate with another reporter to get a bigger story than the one I had. I wasted three hours in your little paper's archive room discovering you reporters didn't care enough about the story the first time to report on it."

I couldn't argue with him there. "Is that why you insulted Ribbon? What do you expect? We're a small town. Carl pushes the envelope, but our subscribers want feel-good stories to balance out the crime. We're not like Philadelphia."

"That's the truth."

The more I talked to Joey, the more solidarity I felt toward Carl. Maybe this was why he'd resisted my Woodward and Bernstein arguments all along. "Listen, Joey, I need to talk to Carl, and he's not returning my calls."

"Kidd, if he hasn't returned your calls, it's probably because he lost access to his phone."

"What happened last night?"

"We got into a, let's call it a disagreement, at the Peanut Bar. The cops arrested us on a drunk and disorderly charge and hauled us into the local county jail."

CHAPTER 35

Journalistic Integrity

"You and Carl were arrested?" I asked.

"Yep." There was pride in Joey's voice. "My paper probably would have bailed Collins out too. We're both working on the Vega murder case, and our owner wouldn't want something like this to get out."

"Who's your owner?"

"Conrad Vega. The media mogul? The father of the guy Suzy Kintz killed? Jeez, Kidd, what kind of a reporter are you?"

I was getting tired of the implications behind that question. "Conrad Vega owns the *Philadelphia Post?*"

"Sure. He owns every paper worth its ink. No offense," he added, though the tone of his voice suggested the offense was intentional. "Collins refused my offer, something about journalistic integrity."

This did not surprise me.

Joey continued. "He said he was going to call you. He said you live to help people. My editor called Vega and arranged bail, and I was out a couple hours after I went in. My wife wasn't happy, and I slept on the sofa, but the sofa might as well have been a bed of angel feathers compared to where I thought I'd be sleeping."

I tuned Joey out. I couldn't get past what Carl had told him about me. If he believed that I lived to help people, then why hadn't he called me?

"I gotta go," I said. I disconnected before Joey could make any more fun of my town.

There'd been no phone calls from Carl. I knew this because there'd been no phone calls from anybody. I'd checked every possible manner in which Nick could have contacted me, and there'd been nothing. Not even a smoke signal.

But there was one more number Carl had for me that I hadn't checked, and that was the paper.

I left Loncar and Bill in Bill's office and stopped by the receptionist's desk. "When my partner finishes up with Mr. Brewster, can you tell him to call me? I received some information related to the case that requires immediate attention."

"Sure," she said.

I hopped into the Cabriolet and peeled out of the lot. The *Ribbon Eagle* wasn't far, and minutes later, I was parked in employee parking. I walked urgently to my desk. Wendy stood when she saw me, holding up both hands to show off an outfit inspired by last month's column on dessert.

"Hi, Samantha! I'm key lime pie!"

I forced a smile and kept moving. There were bigger

issues at hand. I reached the entrance to the bullpen and got two steps in when I realized all this time, Wendy had been asking for my help. She read every one of my columns. She tried to take my advice. She wanted my feedback. And while I'd been busy trying to help the people who didn't ask for it, I'd pacified her with empty compliments that didn't help at all.

I turned around and went back to her desk. "You're a redhead," I said. "You should go with stronger colors. Jewel tones. Emerald green, magenta, sapphire, and amethyst. No matter what I write about in my column, you should always apply that filter."

The smile left her face, and she balled her fists up and crossed her arms over her chest.

I continued. "Your instincts to go with green were right. It's a pretty shade, and you'll get a lot of compliments on it. Do you have any makeup with you?"

She nodded.

"Let's see."

Wendy bent down and pulled a makeup kit out of her handbag. Like a lot of women, she carried around more items than she wore. The cosmetic industry had instilled in women that this was part of being prepared for life: always having options for any occasion on hand.

I picked out a pinkish-peach lipstick and swirled it up, dabbed it on two fingertips, and then dotted it along her cheekbones. The additional color instantly perked up her face. I blended the color into her hairline. "Lips," I said. She parted her lips, and I dabbed the same color into the center of her lower lip and over the bow of her upper. I smacked my lips together to indicate that she should do the same. She mimicked me. I opened her compact and handed it to her. She glanced in and touched her fingers to her cheekbone.

"If you do want to wear pastels, you need a little more color in your face. The lipstick trick works well in a pinch and keeps your whole face coordinated so the colors don't compete with your hair and clothes." I capped the lipstick and handed it back. "Plus, it's easier on your back to carry one lipstick than the whole cosmetic counter."

This time when Wendy smiled, it was genuine.

I left her admiring her reflection in her compact mirror and went to my desk. The message light on my phone was blinking. The Zen of makeup was replaced by anxiety. If the message was from Carl, I'd let him down. If the message was from Nick, well, I just wanted him to call me. I already knew I deserved whatever it was he had to say.

The message was from Carl.

"It's Carl Collins. Listen carefully. Carducci and I got into a fight, and we got arrested. I'm at the county jail in Leesport. He's out on bail. I'm going to spend the night. Do me a favor and tell Monty I'm working on an exclusive about the treatment of prisoners in the system. Tell him to hold editorial space for me. I'll have him something by dead-line. Thanks, Kidd."

He hadn't asked for help. I hadn't let him down. If I'd known, I would have driven straight there and written a check for bail. It never would have occurred to me that Carl would want the experience of spending the night in a cell.

I hung up the phone and went to Monty's office. He

was inside, drinking black coffee and reading something on his computer screen. He waved me in, and I went, closing the door behind me.

"Carl's working on an editorial about the statewide prison system, and he wants you to hold space. He said he'd have it to you by deadline."

"You and Collins got something going?" he asked.

"I'm married!"

"Lots of people are married. Doesn't stop most of them."

"Yeah, well, I'm not most people."

He glanced up from the screen, peering at me over the top of his reading glasses. "That's a new look for you. This part of your column?"

I glanced down at my outfit. I'd forgotten that I wasn't wearing my clothes. Bolstered by Carl's firsthand experience in the prison system, I had an idea. "I found this outfit in Suzy Kintz's storage locker. I thought it could be a good angle for my column: what it's like to be Suzy Kintz, or something like that. You know, walk a mile in her shoes."

"You think wearing her clothes is going to give you a new perspective?"

"I'm driving her car now too," I added. "Every reporter in a five-mile radius is writing about her case these days. You told me to use my connection to her. This is how I do that. I thought it would give me an angle nobody else had."

"Are you planning on getting arrested?"

My face flushed. "No, but I have an inside track on that part too," I said, thinking of Carl.

"Right. You think Carl will cooperate?"

"He told you?" I asked. "I thought I was the only one who knew." Okay. Good. Carl must have called Monty after he called me and let him know what his article was about. "It's his story, but I think he'll tell me what it was like. Knowing Carl, once he's out, he'll want to tell everybody what it was like spending a night in jail."

Monty's face went beet red. "Collins is in jail?" he asked.

I stepped backward instinctively. "You didn't know?"

"Since when?"

"Since yesterday. He left me a message and said he wanted to get the experience for a story."

Monty jumped up from his desk and came toward the door. I stepped to the side to get out of his way. He flung the door open and bellowed, "Wendy!"

Seconds later, Wendy entered the bullpen. The lipstick I'd dotted on her cheeks had been boosted by an internal flush that gave her a rosy, pinkish glow to contrast with her lime-green sweater.

"Collins got himself arrested again. This time he spent the night. Post bail and get him out of there."

Wendy nodded and turned back around. Monty remained in his doorway. "Did anybody else know about this?"

The room went silent. Monty stepped back into his office and slammed the door. I waited until he was back at his desk to ask the one-word question on my mind. "Again?"

Monty shook his head. "Carl thinks getting arrested gives him credibility on the crime beat. We pay the fine and get him out before anything goes on his permanent record." He leaned back. "I don't want to read about this on the news. Does anybody else know about this?"

"Um, you might want to check the *Philadelphia Post*.

Joey Carducci was the other half of the bar fight, and there's a good chance he got home in time to make the early edition."

CHAPTER 36
Carl's Side Project

WORD OF CARL'S NIGHT IN JAIL CIRCULATED THROUGH the bullpen quickly. It was confirmed by Joey's article in the *Post*. A bundle of copies was delivered to the *Ribbon Eagle* along with four dozen more fresh soft pretzels, this time to Carl's attention. Joey Carducci was turning out to be my biggest problem yet.

I pulled six pretzels out of the bag and wrapped them in blank newsprint, stuffed them into my handbag, and left. I called Carl's cell from my walk to the car, from the car, from the road, and from the parking lot I pulled into when I realized I didn't know where I was headed. He answered on the fourth call.

"Monty tricked me," I said in a rush of words. "I was pitching an article about inhabiting Suzy Kintz's world, and he said I had the prison angle covered, and I thought he was talking about you."

"Forget it. I need you to do something for me. Are you near the paper?"

"I'm close," I said, taking the next exit and backtracking the distance I'd driven.

"Go to the archives and tell Andy you're working with me on my project. Ask him for the files I keep down there. He might not believe you at first. I paid him off to lie. Tell him I said you're the most qualified person to assist me."

"Is he going to believe that?"

"Give him the code word. Tell him you're talking about pretzelgate."

"You're kidding."

"Get the files and call me. I can come to your place, but I need a shower first. Your husband won't mind if we work there, will he?"

Nick. Carl's situation had successfully distracted me from the sex tape aftermath, and now I had a choice. Go home and be reminded of the mess I'd made of my personal life or help the person who wanted my assistance. Nick hadn't tried to find me. He said he needed time. It was the only thing in recent memory that he'd ever asked of me, and I wanted him to know I heard his request loud and clear.

"Not my place. Meet me at Suzy Kintz's storage locker on 222."

"See you there."

———

I PARKED and entered the building to the *Ribbon Eagle*, but instead of going through reception like I usually did, I took the elevator down. Andy was at his desk, eating a bologna sandwich on white bread. He was about two thirds of the way through the Updike book and seemed more interested in it than in my unexpected arrival.

"Andy, hi. I just talked to Carl, and he said you were to give me the files for his secret project."

Andy held up his index finger and kept reading.

"He said you might not believe me, and to tell you that I'm the best person to assist him in research."

Andy marked his spot with a bookmark and set the book down. "You kids are all the same. Can't give a man a minute to get to the end of a chapter." He shook his head.

"I don't know if you heard, but Carl spent the night in prison. I'm going to meet up with him now."

Andy didn't react to the news. He also didn't seem particularly concerned that I was asking for Carl's secret files. He took a set of keys and unlocked the bottom drawer of a file cabinet next to his desk. He pulled out a three-inch binder and a thick brown accordion file that was being held closed with a rubber band. He put both on his desk and then sat up. "You have a dolly?"

"For the binder and file? I can carry them," I said.

He pointed to a stack of cardboard boxes in front of him. "What about those?"

I turned my head to the left and assessed the stack. There were four of them stacked on top of each other. I turned my head to the right and assessed the binder and accordion file on Andy's desk. I turned back to the boxes.

"What is this stuff?"

"Carl's research. Back issues of magazines, court transcripts, newspaper clippings, whatever he could find. Carl likes to use the archive room to go through it. Until you came down, I was starting to think he told people the archives were for his use only."

I opened the lid of the top box. Inside were back issues of the music magazine put out by Trenton Vega's group. I closed the lid and turned back to Andy. "Weren't you supposed to ask me for the code word?"

"I called in a favor with my girlfriend at the library to get this stuff. I don't need a code word to decide who gets to take it away. Tell you the truth, the place is starting to feel crowded. Now, if it's all the same to you, I'd like to get back to my book."

I loaded the boxes into the Cabriolet and left. Traffic was light, and I made it to the storage locker quickly. I parked directly in front of the unit and unlocked the gate then went to the clothing rack to find something more suitable for digging around old files than an ivory ponte knit two-piece dress. On the back of the rack, I found a pair of faded men's jeans and a crested blazer. I ducked behind the rolling rack and pulled the jeans on, removed my skirt and draped it over the rack, and then pulled the top over my head and slipped into the blazer. I buttoned it up, aware that without a shirt underneath I was working my cleavage more than I'd like. I opened and shut a couple of boxes and found a stack of folded T-shirts. Carl's 1966 pale-yellow Mustang convertible pulled up behind the Cabriolet just as I slipped the blazer off. I yanked the top T-shirt over my bra, put the blazer back on, and came out from behind the rack.

Carl looked slightly worse for wear after his night in jail. As promised, he'd taken a shower, and his hair was still damp. Instead of his usual uniform of seersucker suit, white shirt, and blue necktie, he had on a dark-green sweatshirt that said MIDDLETON PREP ACADEMY and jeans with a broken-in pair of Stan Smiths.

"Nice blazer," he said, as if this were just another day and we were going to engage in small talk. I was so happy to see him that instead of responding to the compliment, I threw my arms around him. His return hug was tentative.

I stood back. "I'm sorry I pushed you to collaborate with Joey Carducci. I thought it would be good for Suzy's case, you two pooling resources. I didn't stop to think about anything else. I should have listened—"

Carl pushed me away. "Jeez, Kidd. Calm down. Did you and your husband have a fight or something? It was one night in county jail. It'll make a good chapter in my book."

"What book?"

"The true crime book I'm writing about Suzy Kintz. Didn't Andy tell you? I've been collecting info on her since her initial arrest."

I considered what I'd found out about Suzy since being notified of the requested visit, about the memories I had from high school and the details I'd picked up since then. Compared to this, they were the tip of the iceberg.

"What's your connection to Suzy?" I asked.

"She's newsworthy."

I shook my head. "There has to be more than that. You've amassed a couple of decades' worth of material. I've heard about this happening with reporters. There's one story that gets into your blood, and that's the one you follow for your whole career. This isn't just a piece of news to you. It's your career-defining story. It's why you were so mad when I wanted to share info with Joey Carducci. It's probably why you two got into a fight."

"Carducci is a putz."

"I can help you," I said but quickly added, "but you have to tell me what you need. I want to find out the truth."

"You want to get Suzy out?"

"If she didn't commit the crime."

"You think there's a chance she did?"

"I'm willing to consider all sides of the story, not just hers."

Carl tipped his head and assessed me for a moment. After a few seconds, he nodded as if I'd passed a test. He pointed to my blazer. "Where'd you get the blazer?"

"I, um, borrowed it."

"I didn't think you went to Middleton. I would have known."

I felt my face scrunch up in confusion. I pointed to his sweatshirt. "Middleton Prep? Is that where this jacket is from?"

"Sure. It was part of our uniform."

An image came back to me. The picture of Suzy in a ball skirt made from mismatched plaid shirts from Goodwill. She'd paired it with this jacket, collar up, belted at the waist. That was before she adopted her daily uniform of black suit and white T-shirt. "Why are you asking about my blazer?"

"I guess I've been thinking about those days a lot lately. That's when I first met Suzy. I didn't exactly meet her, though. She used to come to the school during lunch to eat with her boyfriend. He was a senior. I was a freshman. People said she'd been expelled, and that made her mysterious."

"What do you remember about her?"

"Not a lot, but there was this one day. The visitor spaces were full, so she parked in the faculty lot. The dean came out and told her to move her car. She didn't put up a fight. Before she left, she asked which car was his, and he pointed out a navy-blue BMW. She left. A couple of minutes later, a truck pulled into the lot, and a guy booted the dean's car. I saw the whole thing because I forgot my textbook and had to go back to my dorm room to get it before class. The story about the boot spread through the school by the end of the day, but nobody else knew who was responsible. I wrote an article about it for the Middleton Prep Newspaper and went from being a nobody freshman to a reporter overnight."

"Was there any fallout?"

"I was a little worried about the boyfriend, but he turned out to be cool. He gave me a copy of the paper with a note on it: 'Nice reporting. -Suzy'."

It seemed I wasn't the only person to have a Suzy Kintz story. It could have been written off to the cult of celebrity: the attention she received for killing her husband made her famous and having a connection to her meant a little of that fame rubbed off on us too. But there was something else. From the first day she walked into homeroom and the teacher seated her behind me, from every time the teacher accidentally called me Samantha Kintz or called her Susanna Kidd, from the way she taught me eye shadow application or talked art with Eddie or complimented Carl on his first news story, she had a way of silently encouraging us. By making her advisory role no big deal, she gently allowed us to see what we could do and then do it.

I could understand how the story had made an impression on Carl. Not only because of Suzy's encouragement, but because here was a girl who was rumored to have been kicked out of the school. She didn't throw a fit when the dean told her to move her car, but she didn't just walk away, either. To a ninth grader, watching Suzy have the dean's car booted must have been like watching Batgirl prank Police Commissioner Gordon.

"Did Suzy come to the school much after that?"

"No. She and her boyfriend broke up. I heard his parents got wind of the story and thought she was trouble. Kinda figures, I guess. That family is probably overly sensitive when it comes to cars."

"Why?"

"They own the biggest dealer in Ribbon. Tanner Auto?"

"Suzy Kintz's high school boyfriend at Middleton Prep was Kent Tanner?"

"Yes. Why?"

"Wait here while I change. You just gave me an idea."

CHAPTER 37
A Whole New Angle

How had I not considered this? Suzy said her sister had invited an old friend, and she needed anti-anxiety medicine to manage her mental state. That meant more than just a casual acquaintance. I'd spent memory lane preoccupied with the Suzy I knew from Ribbon High, but she'd had a life before being kicked out of prep school, and if my new suspicion was correct, I was about to learn more about it. Kent Tanner represented a whole new angle.

I hopped behind the rolling rack and quickly traded the blazer, T-shirt, and jeans for the ivory ponte knit ensemble. It was one thing for Carl to be wearing a Middleton Prep Academy sweatshirt; Kent would recognize him. But me wearing what I suspected was his blazer was going to tip my hand more than I'd like. Especially since I was driving Suzy's car.

I came out from behind the rack and grabbed my bag. "Come on," I said. As soon as Carl was out of the storage unit, I slammed the gate down and locked the padlock.

"Not that I don't love a hot lead, but are you going to tell me where we're going?"

"Tanner Auto," I said.

"I already tried to interview Kent," Carl said, barely keeping up with me as I sped toward the Cabriolet. "Unless you have a way to get to him that I don't, he doesn't want to talk about her."

I unlocked the doors and got into the driver's seat. "Get in," I said.

"Holy shit, Kidd. Is that her car?"

———

THE DRIVE to Tanner Auto was quick. I pulled into the lot and drove slowly around the perimeter of the show-room, parking in a space visible from Kent's office. Carl unhooked his seatbelt, and I put my hand on his arm. "Wait. I want to give Kent time to recognize the car and start to wonder about it before he sees me get out."

My plan worked. I readjusted the rearview mirror and watched Kent Tanner exit the showroom. He stood a few feet in front of the door, staring at the license plate. He shielded his eyes and scanned the lot and then buttoned his blazer and advanced toward us.

"Okay, now."

I unclicked my seatbelt and got out of the car. I smiled broadly. "Kent. Hi." I pointed the remote at the car and locked it. "Do you remember Carl Collins? We're friends from the paper."

"Hey, Kent," Carl said. For a moment, I saw the

dynamic that must have existed between ninth-grade Carl and twelfth-grade Kent.

"Where did you get this car?" Kent asked.

"I borrowed it from a mutual friend."

By this time, Kent and I were face to face. I didn't know what to expect aside from surprise on his part, a prediction he'd already fulfilled.

"How is she?" he asked. There was nothing behind his question, no wistfulness, no anger, no hostility, no regret. It was just a question, asked in the same tone of voice he might have used to ask about the transmission. "I read your article in the paper. 'What she was like in high school.' You captured her spirit with that memory."

"She's in prison for life, that's how she is. Have you ever tried to visit her? Contact her? She was moved back to Ribbon years ago. She's in your back yard."

"Why would I visit her? She's an old girlfriend. We were kids. She graduated and we went separate ways. I got my business degree at Penn and started working at the dealership. In high school, everybody seems the same. Once you're out, you realize it was just the illusion of the uniform." He glanced at Carl's sweatshirt.

"You and Suzy didn't keep in touch?" I asked.

He shrugged. "It didn't seem worth it. Once she left, the world she inhabited blew up. I'm happy living here with my wife and kids. The dealership keeps me busy." He looked at Carl again and then back to me. "Is this conversation on the record? Am I going to read about your ambush in tomorrow's paper?"

I turned to Carl. "Do me a favor? Go inside and get me a cup of coffee."

Carl recognized that it was better to get information than to get a quote. He nodded and left us alone. I waited until he was inside the showroom to turn back to Kent. "You wouldn't have asked that question unless you had something more to say."

He looked out at the road while cars zinged past. "I was supposed to be at dinner that night," he said. "I ran into her sister, and she invited me. I thought it was going to be a group of friends, but when I got to the restaurant and saw that car, I just — I didn't want to deal with the small talk. We were pretty close when we were teenagers, but things got harder after she got kicked out of Middleton." He pointed inside. "Did Carl tell you about the boot on the dean's car?"

"Yes."

"My dad sold the dean that car. When my parents found out Suzy was responsible, they told me to stop seeing her. That made it exciting at first, but she was, I don't know, always somewhere else. Like she left before she left. We broke up, and I heard she took off for Europe, when she graduated, and aside from the newspapers, I never saw her again."

"What did you do about the dinner?" I asked.

"I drove around for a while to clear my head. I didn't know if her sister told her I was going to be there, but after a while, not showing up felt petty. Like I was holding a grudge. I figured dinner would be over by then, so I drove out to the Kintz house. I didn't see her car, so I left."

Every time I talked to someone about Suzy, I had a strange feeling, like we were connected by this person who'd touched our lives. It illustrated how easy it is to influence someone without even trying. Social media had created a world where "influencer" was a job title and people vied for attention every day, but before chat rooms and personal profiles and unboxing videos and memes, Suzy played to the audience in front of her and became what we wanted to see.

"Was she for real?" I asked Kent. His eyes narrowed slightly, and I took his silence as a need to clarify my question. "Was she genuine, or was it all an act? She's nothing like her family. The aloof, untouchable girl who didn't care about authority and followed her own compass point. It sounds like you knew her better than most people, or at least you did back then."

"Suzy's best trait was that she didn't care about anything. It was also her worst. It made her wild and free and curious, but it also made it impossible to establish a deep and meaningful connection. We had fun, and when you're sixteen and you fall in love with a person who becomes your whole world, you think you hit the lottery. It wasn't until after we broke up that I realized how empty our time together was."

I felt Kent had said all he wanted to say on the matter of Suzy Kintz, but I had one last question. Before he could completely close the door on the conversation, I asked it. "Do you think she killed her husband?"

He shifted his attention back to me. I held his gaze.

"On the record? No comment."

"And off the record?"

"Knowing how she was back then, I wouldn't be surprised."

CHAPTER 38

The Local Pretzel Consortium

I thanked Kent for his time and promised to decide on a car purchase soon. I hadn't expected my vehicular problems to bleed into the rest of my life, but thanks to Suzy's request that I visit her in prison, everything had become one big mess with her at the center. Just about the only thing I couldn't blame on her was my fight with Nick. I'd created that mess all on my own.

I found Carl inside the showroom, making a pot of coffee in the waiting room. He pointed to the news. "Kintz Pretzels has been closed indefinitely."

I'd forgotten all about the equipment malfunction. "There was an explosion in the factory," I said. "I was there."

"Well, get this. The confession from the prisoner at Rikers Island brought new attention to Suzy's case. Kintz pretzel sales dropped in half this week. The insurance investigators reported that it wasn't an accident. Someone tampered with the machine."

I remembered the sad, earnest energy that exuded from

Tom and Katy Kintz. These were people who'd had too many setbacks. When I first started looking into Suzy's case, I pictured her life as pretzel heiress, the trust fund recipient who took off for Europe the night of high school graduation. I'd believed that her life had been easy because she never had to say no because of money. But her life came with troubles I couldn't imagine.

Her family, who'd stood by her all these years, had become a target of the community because of her. If she hadn't killed her husband, then she'd given up half of her life because someone else did. Her willingness to accept the punishment and never talk to the press was like a white flag of surrender. She never claimed innocence, and she never claimed remorse. Maybe being Suzy Kintz had been more than she could bear, and she let go of the promise of her future to clock time behind the walls of a correctional facility.

On the TV monitor, a reporter stood in front of Kintz Pretzels. While she talked, a van from a competing pretzel company pulled in behind her. The driver got out and opened up the back, and with the help of the person from the passenger side, carried cartons into the store. A second van for a second pretzel company pulled in, and this time four people got out and unloaded. The reporter, who appeared to be using a tripod and a cell phone to film her segment, walked away from her camera and approached the newcomers. After a brief exchange, she came back to her spot.

"Well, here's some bright Ribbon, Pennsylvania news for you. The local pretzel consortium has pulled together to support the Kintz family. They'll be selling their pretzels from inside while the Kintz equipment is being repaired and donating one hundred percent of the sales from this location to the Kintz pretzel business."

"How do you like that," Carl said. "They just showed up to help without being asked."

I waited for Carl to add the inevitable "just like you," but Carl didn't know me that way. He'd never been on the receiving end of my plan to help him. Maybe that was why, after the fallout with Nick, instead of spending my day with a friend who would listen to my woes, I was spending it with someone I otherwise considered a nuisance.

"Let's go," I said. "We can make it there in less than fifteen minutes."

"Where? Kintz Pretzels?" Carl dismissed the idea. "That story's already old. Monty either sent a cub reporter or had someone write up a piece based on the news. Our story is still Suzy Kintz. Did she or didn't she? You're the one with the exclusive interview with her high school ex. Are you using it in your 'Who She Was in High School' series?"

"No. I'm out. I don't know if she did or didn't, and I'm starting not to care." I pointed to the screen. "Her family's troubles started the night Trenton Vega was murdered in their guest cottage. And look at what's happening today. The pretzel community showed up. They're standing by the Kintzes. It's what a community does best. They're there for each other, even when they're not asked."

My voice cracked. I wasn't talking about a community; I was justifying my instincts. But the problem was on the news, the generosity of the pretzel company was going to balloon into goodwill and positive publicity. The companies who donated their pretzels to help out the Kintzes would get that back tenfold after the story broke. They weren't doing it out of the goodness of their hearts. It wasn't like me and Nick at all.

Except it was. Helping Nick with publicity *was* all about me. It was me inserting myself into his business. It was me being able to manipulate a thank you. It was me undermining how he ran his business. It was me getting a cute story to tell people later in life. *Hey honey, remember that time I did that thing so you could become famous? Tell them what I did. Sure, honey. You're going to love this. Back when I was just starting my sneaker business, my wife got the idea to leak a private video to the media. That's right. Classic Samantha.*

I was keeping the story all about me, and that was all anybody would remember. Not the success of Nick's sneaker line. Not his talent as a designer. Not his business acumen, or celebrity endorsements, or creative advertising strategies. I'd be the center of attention, and nobody would look elsewhere.

I felt, rather than knew, that I wasn't the only person in my life who knew how to be the center of attention. Suzy Kintz had successfully defined that role in her formative years. That sociopathic behavior wasn't about popularity, it was about diversion. If people paid attention to her, then they weren't paying attention to someone else. Until one night, in the guest cottage of her parents' compound on the outskirts of Ribbon, Pennsylvania seventeen years ago, they were.

I couldn't believe I'd missed it.

CHAPTER 39

Beyond Mere Acquaintances

"WE NEED TO GO," I SAID. I LEFT THE TANNER AUTO showroom and approached the Cabriolet. I unlocked the car and was inside with the engine running before Carl had his door closed.

"Where to?"

"Berks County Correctional Facility for Females," I said.

"Do you have a visit scheduled?"

"No. Suzy's visitation privileges were revoked after she picked a fight with another prisoner. This story isn't about the pretzel companies, it's about her incarceration in Berks County. None of this happened when she was in the maximum-security prison in — what town was that?"

"Muncy."

"Right. Muncy. Nobody cared about her story all these years, and now this. Deathbed confession from a prisoner in Rikers brought attention back to the case, and then *boom*. The model prisoner who doesn't talk to the press gets into a fight? In seventeen years, she's never had an altercation.

She's pulling the heat back onto her. She didn't kill her husband, but she knows who did. Maybe she's scared of what they'll do to her family, and this is the best way for her to protect them." And the more people paid attention to her family, the bigger her maneuvers were going to have to be to divert attention and keep them safe.

I was happy to have Carl along for the ride, and not just because he wasn't aware that underscoring my motivation to get at the truth was the desire to not think about my fallout with Nick.

Carl was an expert in Suzy's case. He'd been following every detail for seventeen years. He had cartons of accumulated research. He wasn't in the car because of anything I offered to give him, but because his book needed an ending.

I pulled into the BCCFF parking lot and parked in a space on the lower level. Together, we walked to the entrance. Women in khaki work uniforms were outside the building, tending to the grounds, while the large prison guard who'd patted me down supervised them. She frowned when I approached. I smiled and waved like we were old friends (she *had* touched my privates during the pat-down, at least some of them, and that meant we were beyond mere acquaintances).

"I can get you in the front door," I said to Carl, "but after that, you're on your own. Say whatever you want to say and do whatever you want to do. You're the investigative reporter." We entered the facility and approached the front desk. "Hi," I said. "I'm Samantha Kidd. I'm here to see Peter Genovese about Suzy Kintz's treatment. Can I have a locker key?"

Carl whispered in my ear, "Who's Peter Genovese?"

I whispered back, "The treatment director."

I took the key and put my handbag in the locker. Before I closed it, I turned the burner phone on record and set it in front of my bag. I didn't expect to bust a prison scandal wide open with my convenient possession of the burner phone, but I also wasn't willing to sit around wondering what conversations took place when no one was watching. I locked up the locker just as the treatment director rounded the corner.

Today Peter Genovese's cheap suit was gray. The shoulder seams puckered, and the absence of buttons by the cuffs indicated an off-the-rack job. Wardrobe wasn't an investment item for him; he probably tore through a couple suits a year. His silver hair had been cut since the day of the press conference, this time neatly framing out his ears and face.

"Samantha Kidd, is it?" he asked. "From the *Ribbon Eagle*."

"You remembered." I held out my hand and shook his. "This is Carl Collins. He's an investigative reporter. We'd like to talk about the treatment of Suzy Kintz."

"I don't understand," he said, looking back and forth between our faces. A ruddy shade of pink colored his cheeks.

"That's the point," I said. "You have a model prisoner who's never once had an altercation with another inmate or employee of the prison, and after news that could possibly exonerate her, you put her in solitary confinement. I think the subscribers of our paper would like to hear the reasoning behind that choice of treatment." I turned to Carl. "Don't you?"

Carl agreed.

Peter held both hands up in protest. "Who told you Suzy was in solitary confinement?"

"Don't worry about our source," I said with mounting confidence. "These scandals have a way of getting out. Do you want to continue this conversation in the hallway or in your office?"

"Ms. Kidd, we can continue it anywhere you'd like, but I need to correct your misinformation. Suzy Kintz isn't in solitary confinement. She's never been in solitary confinement. Right now she's in the visitor lounge."

"Can I meet with her?"

"You can, but your friend can't." He turned to Carl. "That's not an indictment on Ms. Kintz or on your credentials with the newspaper. It's policy. Visitors have to be screened. You can wait in your car."

"How about a tour?" Carl said.

———

I LEFT Carl with the treatment director and went through the sign-in/pat-down stages of my visit, all the while questioning why Bill Brewster had lied to me about Suzy's availability. He'd said she revoked my visitation rights. And when I questioned that, he said she was in solitary confinement for initiating an altercation with another prisoner. Neither action felt authentic to the Suzy I'd met with on my two visits, but I'd believed him. And now, no matter what angle I attacked that question from, I couldn't find an answer.

As I followed the prison guard through the hallway, I

thought about all the questions I hadn't asked. This was a world that ran on rules. Visitation took place after a series of steps were followed. The second time I was here, my visit had been cut short, not because of anything Suzy or I had done, but because Eddie had gotten out of his car and wandered the exterior of the building. I couldn't imagine what it was like to live in here, blindly following the policies and procedures laid out by the powers that be. I'd been exposed to murderers in the past and believed that actions have consequences, but walking through these halls, I couldn't ignore what freedoms had been lost by the prisoners. It was chilling.

We reached the doors to the visitation lounge, and the guard entered first. When I stepped out from behind her, I saw that today, the room was bustling. Most of the small round tables were occupied, women and kids, women and men, women and other women. There was a low hum of conversation occasionally punctuated by laughter. Nobody seemed to notice that we'd entered. Aside from the sheer number of women wearing prison-issue faded gray sweats, this could have been a café filled with girl bosses having a weekly strategy meeting with their staff.

"Kintz!" the prison guard called.

Suzy stood from a chair on the far left side of the room. I held my hand up in a wave. *Act cool, Samantha. This isn't high school.*

"Go on," the guard said.

I thanked her and made my way around the perimeter of the room. As I got closer, I saw that Suzy was visiting with her sister, Dawn. I approached their table and put my hand on the back of an empty chair.

"Hi," I said to them both.

Suzy leaned back. "Samantha," she said. "I didn't think you were going to come back."

"That wasn't my fault," I said. "I've learned a lot since my last visit." I glanced at Dawn's face. She'd been crying. She caught my eyes for a fleeting second and then averted them to the table. I'd been hoping to catch Suzy alone and talk through the disconnected facts I'd found. Interrupting an emotional family reunion wasn't on the agenda. "I'm sorry to intrude," I said.

"Dawn, get me some cigarettes, would you?" Suzy said. Dawn left us alone at the table. "Sit down. Talk. How much have you figured out?"

Until five minutes ago, I wasn't sure I'd figured out anything. All I'd known was that people were lying. But there was something about the way Dawn had looked at me when I stood by the table.

Correction: how she looked at my outfit.

I was wearing the ivory ponte knit two-piece dress I'd found amongst Suzy's belongings, the one that had been under the dry-cleaning plastic, the one that had been dropped off the night after the murder on a rush job and hung with the rest of Suzy's things for seventeen years in a storage locker.

"It was Dawn," I said. And for the first time since I'd met Suzy Kintz, her expression softened, and I knew there was one person she cared about more than herself, and she'd sacrificed her life to protect her.

CHAPTER 40
Code

"This isn't your outfit, is it?" I asked.

"It was. I loaned it to my sister once and never saw it again."

"Because she wore it the night Trenton Vega was murdered." I felt like I was standing in the middle of a whirlpool of colors that was coalescing into shapes and forms, making sense out of abstractness, defining moments I'd learned about but hadn't fully understood.

"You were in the shower when she shot him," I said. "Just like you told the detectives."

Suzy raised her eyebrows, neither a confirmation nor a denial. I turned my head toward the concession stand but didn't see Dawn.

"She left," Suzy said.

"You asked her for cigarettes."

"Code. She's probably on Route 222 by now."

I pushed my chair away from the table to stand. My sudden movement caught the attention of the prison guard by the door. She scanned the tables in our area, unsure which one she should be watching. I dropped my eyes to the women who filled the tables between us and her: in the eyes of the state, they were criminals serving time for crimes committed, but today, they were wives, sisters, daughters, friends.

I turned back to face Suzy. "I know Dawn killed Trenton Vega. I also know he almost put you in the hospital at least once. You said it yourself. You don't leave a man like Trenton Vega without a plan. What I don't know — what I want you to tell me is how long the two of you planned his murder."

I leaned forward, propped on my forearms, staring Suzy directly in the eyes. I'd been here twice, and twice I'd been distracted by memories of the girl I admired in high school. The girl who seemed untouchable, who acted according to her personal code and got away with nonconformity. I'd been drawn into her orbit, not because she actively pulled me in, but because she appeared to need nothing. No one. Suzy Kintz had been an island, and in a sea of high school students who were obsessed with fitting in, her self-isolation made her a novelty.

"You came to Ribbon by yourself," I said. "I know that much. You drove your Audi to dinner and took a car service home. You went upstairs and took a shower, giving Dawn enough time to come in after you and kill Trenton."

She leaned back, her relaxed body language in complete contrast to my earnest posture. She didn't deny anything I said. She nodded once, as if I was on the right track, but didn't contribute to the narrative.

"You arranged for the gun to be in the nightstand. If you're familiar with guns, then your sister probably was too.

That was the plan, wasn't it? You left alone and went home and got into the shower. Dawn waited for Trenton to get there. He was too strong for one of you to subdue him, but both of you could have —"

"He thought she was me," Suzy said quietly. A flicker of something — defiance? – crossed her face. Her voice remained even. She glanced at my torso. "Trenton bought me that outfit. He hated that I wore men's suits and wanted me to dress differently. I'd left that outfit in the closet here, and when Dawn asked if she could borrow it, I thought why not?" Her eyes moved from my torso to my face. "He was high on coke, which wasn't new, but that night, he was worse than usual. He thought she was me," she repeated. "He grabbed her hair, and she screamed. I heard her and got out of the shower and found them in the bedroom. When he saw me, he realized his mistake. He threw her onto the bed and came at me. I remember wanting to run away, but I had to make sure Dawn was safe. And then a gun fired, and Trenton collapsed against me and fell onto the floor."

"You told Dawn to leave," I guessed. "You waited for her to get out of the house before you called 911." She nodded. "That's why the police never took this outfit. That's why she was able to drop it off at the cleaner's the next day."

"She told me about that," Suzy said. "She wanted to get it back into the closet in case someone knew it was missing. I told her to move all of my stuff into a storage locker so no one would know what was there and what wasn't." She pointed to the outfit. "I received a lot of samples from designers from working for *Luxe Magazine*," she said. "That storage locker is filled with clothes that have never been worn. Why'd you notice that one?"

"I could tell it had recently been dry cleaned. I wanted to know which dry cleaner you trusted with your clothes."

It was an embarrassing confession. I'd spent time in the archives of the paper. Time digging through a storage locker, uncovering medical reports, exposing suspects, tracking down leads, and collaborating with a member of a competing news outlet, and it had been the same old envy I'd felt of Suzy in high school that drew my attention to this garment. And if I'd never wanted to know who she trusted with her dry cleaning, I might never have gotten the story I'd heard today.

It was a great story. The kind that made journalism careers. And I knew exactly which journalist would tell it.

———

Two DAYS LATER, the details surrounding the night of Trenton Vega's murder covered the front page of the *Ribbon Eagle*. Byline: Carl Collins, with additional reporting from Samantha Kidd. I'd tried to refuse the credit but he insisted. I clipped the article and added it to my scrapbook.

In time, forensic scientists would pull Trenton Vega's clothes from an evidence locker and swab them for fibers, which they would find, fibers that matched those from the ivory ponte knit outfit. It fit with Dawn Kintz's story that Trenton Vega had made physical contact with her and fit with the idea that he'd mistaken her for her sister. Photos of Dawn Kintz from seventeen years ago confirmed the similarity in appearance between the two sisters. When Suzy was convicted, the stress of the secret had taken its toll on Dawn. She'd put on weight quickly, and within a year looked like an entirely different person.

Carl tracked down the Greenwich Village medical center and matched official reports with the document I'd found in Suzy's belongings. She'd kept the copy she took hidden amongst her things, a possible security blanket if he ever tried to hurt her again, but she hadn't counted on the staff documenting the abuse after she left or the unofficial records being transferred to film when the hospital went digital.

Any questions I had about Bill Brewster's honesty were dismissed when I learned who'd been on the other end of the suspicious phone call: Joey Carducci. After the fight that got the two reporters arrested, Joey started flipping rocks to find out what information he'd missed. The outfit had been the last thing we'd spoke about and he ran with it, not knowing (like me) that it was the least important piece of the puzzle.

Joey may have gotten tripped up on details of no consequence, but I had to hand it to Carl. He did an excellent piece of investigative reporting, starting the very day I was in the prison lounge getting a confession from Suzy. He recognized Dawn Kintz when she left. He followed her to the parking lot and confronted her, initially just looking for a quote. But while I was floating my story to Suzy for confirmation, Carl was getting a first-hand exclusive from Dawn. When the prisoner in Rikers Island confessed to the unrelated murder of the hiker found eight miles from the Kintz family compound, Dawn wanted to come forward and tell the truth about what happened that night. She believed public opinion had shifted and the time was right. Suzy disagreed. It wasn't worth it, she'd told her sister. I won't take a chance on you paying for a mistake I made.

It was Dawn who'd kept up with the registration and maintenance on the Cabriolet.

It was Dawn who claimed to have my visitation rights revoked.

And it was Dawn who rigged the main pretzel oven at Kintz Pretzels to break down. Detective Loncar scared her when he showed up asking questions. She'd been so rattled that she created a distraction. It was the closest she'd come to a confession before I figured it all out.

While Carl captivated the Ribbon, Pennsylvania subscriber base (circulation was up twenty-three percent!), I cleaned up my mess. After leaving the prison and dropping Carl off at the storage locker where he'd left his car, I drove the white Audi Cabriolet to Tanner Auto, asked if they could return it to the Kintz compound, and drove away in the GR Supra A91 Edition in Refraction blue that I'd recommended to Loncar.

I drove home and parked in the driveway next to Nick's white truck. I went inside and found him in the living room, sitting on the sofa, with my shiny pink folder with the kitten on the front in his hands.

He held up the folder. "Is this what I think it is?"

"What do you think it is?"

"Not now, Kidd. Is this — are these directorial notes about making a sex tape to help me get publicity?"

I stood awkwardly in the doorway. "I can explain."

He opened the folder and read from my notes. "'Make sure Nick looks good. Risqué, not raunchy. Don't be self-conscious. Take Jodie Foster Masterclass on filmmaking. Go on juice diet. *Stop eating pretzels."* He held up the sheet of paper, and I saw my handwriting. "Did you really watch a Masterclass on filmmaking?"

"Not the whole class. Jodie says you should be open to improvisation, and I didn't think this was the kind of film you storyboard."

Nick stifled a smile. "You were serious about this, weren't you?"

I shrugged.

"Sit down, Samantha."

I crossed the room and lowered myself onto the sofa with two feet of space between us. "I had good intentions," I said.

"You always have good intentions. That's not the point."

"Then what is?"

"You have to let me live my life too," he said. "You have to let me figure out how to get publicity. I appreciate that you want me to look good, but that's my problem. Do you understand that?"

"I learned my lesson," I said. "Your business is your business, and I'm done offering unsolicited help. If you want my input, you'll have to ask me."

"Is that a promise?"

"Do you promise to ask?"

He opened his arms up and pulled me into an embrace. "You're my secret weapon, Kidd, I just don't want you to wear yourself out. When I need you, I promise I'll ask."

Epilogue

DURING THE PRESS CONFERENCE FOLLOWING SUZY Kintz's clemency hearing, a box arrived from China. I carried it to the basement, where Nick had set up a home office. Logan was sprawled out in front of Nick's printer.

"Thanks," Nick said. He set the box behind him and went back to his computer.

"You're not going to open it?"

"Not right now," he said.

"But it's from China. It's a sample, isn't it? A prototype?"

"It can wait."

A new memory surfaced, one from the days when I was a shoe buyer for Bentley's. No matter what we were doing in the office, when samples arrived, we dropped everything and opened them. We treated packages like presents that might go away if left unattended.

That was my memory. Like the memories of Suzy that had come back to me since the press conference. It was how I did things. Before Suzy, I might have grabbed the box cutter and opened the package for Nick. I might have pestered him to drop everything and show me what he designed. I might have sat down and waited, forcing him to alter his agenda to entertain me. But I'd made a promise, and even though we all knew there was a strong chance I'd break it someday, I'd like to say I made it more than a month.

"Okay," I said. "I'm going upstairs to work on a column for the paper. Want to get a pizza later?"

"Sure," he said. He didn't look up.

I scooped up Logan and scratched his ears. He rearranged himself in my arms and put his paws over my shoulder. I kissed the top of his head and carried him up two flights of stairs to my office. I'd given Suzy's files to Carl, and now, the room felt spacious. I set Logan on my desk, and he jumped down, meowed, and left. I live-streamed the press conference and watched Suzy Kintz get out of prison, her shiny, olive-oil-conditioned hair in place, her gray prison sweats looking like something from Saks. I shut down the computer and spent the next hour staring out my window, thinking about the similarities between me and Suzy Kintz. Suzy had helped her sister by serving seventeen years for a murder she hadn't committed. I doubted it was a favor her sister had requested.

Suzy's charges were downgraded to accessory to murder and time served. She was granted clemency and released. I let Carl cover the press conference while I spent the day at home. A month and a day into my resolve not to help people who didn't ask for help first, Nick asked my opinion on his sneaker designs.

And just like that, a new door opened.

About the Author

National bestselling author Diane Vallere writes smart, funny, and fashionable character-based mysteries. After two decades working for a top luxury retailer, she traded fashion accessories for accessories to murder. A past president of Sisters in Crime, Diane started her own detective agency at age ten and has maintained a passion for shoes, clues, and clothes ever since. Find out more at dianevallere.com.

Acknowledgments

At separate times, I have described the Samantha Kidd mysteries as about fashion and about personal growth, but I could just as easily said they were about pretzels. Set in a fictionalized version of Reading, Pennsylvania, arguably the pretzel capital of the world, it would be difficult to create a character who doesn't include pretzels as part of her everyday life. Samantha Kidd is the character in question, and she doesn't just eat pretzels. She loves pretzels. Not one book has gone by without her enjoying a Little Cheeser, an Extra Dark, a baldie, or a soft pretzel—or in the case of *Panty Raid*, lamenting the lack of good pretzels in Las Vegas.

When it came time to imagine Samantha's next adventure, inspired mildly by true-crime stories on *Forensic Files* and the podcast *Serial*, I thought it would be interesting if she got involved in a case that happened in the past. Samantha's world being about her having moved back to the town where she grew up, it was a natural to make the suspected criminal someone she once knew. The words "pretzel heiress" pretty much typed themselves while I was free-writing concepts for the book, and the idea sounded like so much fun that I ran with it.

It's no exaggeration to say this book was powered by pretzels, but it was also benefitted from the support of my writer group: Gigi Pandian, Ellen Byron, and Lisa Matthews, my close friend Jordaina Sydney Robinson, and my readers: subscribers of the Weekly DiVa. Thanks also to my parents, Mary Vallere and Donald Vallere, who are a consistent source of support.

The book also benefitted from the vlogs of women who spent some time in prison: Christina Randall, Sydhip, and Jessica Kent, none of whom I know personally, but each of whom share their accounts of life inside prison on YouTube, which gave me flavor for Suzy Kintz's experience. Sometimes days of research find its way into only one or two sentences, but that doesn't diminish their value.

To the members of the Polyester Posse, the first people to read the whole book, thank you!

And to everyone who suggested a car for Samantha Kidd: thank you! You had her driving Mini Coopers, Mustangs, Mazda Miatas, Jaguars, Audis, Porsches, T-birds, pink Rolls Royces, SUVs, Beetles, Mercedes, Cadillacs, electric cars, classic cars, sports cars, Smart Cars, and more. I loved hearing how you reached your choice, equal parts "Samantha needs to go unnoticed" to "Samantha needs to stand out," and probably my personal fave, "Samantha needs a place to put all those shoes." You know her well!

Also By

With Vics You Get Eggroll

The Decorator Who Knew Too Much

The Pajama Frame

Lover Come Hack

Apprehend Me No Flowers

Teacher's Threat

The Kill of It All

Love Me or Grieve Me

Please Don't Push Up the Daisies

Sylvia Stryker Outer Space Mysteries

Murder on a Moon Trek

Scandal on a Moon Trek

Hijacked on a Moon Trek

Framed on a Moon Trek

Material Witness Mysteries

Suede to Rest

Crushed Velvet

Silk Stalkings

Tulle Death Do Us Part

Costume Shop Mystery Series

A Disguise to Die For

Masking for Trouble

Dressed to Confess